PENGUIN BOOKS

EM AND THE BIG HOOM

Jerry Pinto is a writer of prose, poetry, and children's fiction, as well as being a journalist. *Em and the Big Hoom,* winner of the 2013 Crossword Book Award and the Hindu Literary Award, is his first novel. He lives in Mumbai, India.

Em and the Big Hoom

JERRY PINTO

PENGUIN BOOKS

PENGUIN BOOKS
Published by the Penguin Group
Penguin Group (USA) LLC
375 Hudson Street
New York, New York 10014

USA | Canada | UK | Ireland | Australia | New Zealand | India | South Africa | China
penguin.com
A Penguin Random House Company

First published in India by Aleph Book Company 2012
First published in Great Britain by Viking 2014
Published in Penguin Books (USA) 2014

LIBRARY OF CONGRESS CATALOGING-IN-PUBLICATION DATA
Pinto, Jerry.
Em and the Big Hoom : a novel / Jerry Pinto.
pages cm
ISBN 978-0-14-312476-4 (paperback)
1. Women--Fiction.   2. Manic-depressive illness—Fiction.   3. Domestic fiction.   I. Title.
PR9499.4.P56E43 2014
823'.92—dc23   2014005738

Printed in the United States of America
1   3   5   7   9   10   8   6   4   2

Set in Dante MT Std

Contents

'Someone turned on a tap'

Dear Angel Ears,

Outside the window, a Marathi manus is asking mournfully if anyone would like to buy salt. Or at least that's what I think. Mee-ee-et, he wails, Me-eeetwallah, mee-eet. Other sounds: Mae mumbling about morning Mass; an impertinent sparrow demanding the last bit of my toast.

I miss you terribly. But if you are going to send me a postcard, I shall abstain. I think postcards are for acquaintances and now that we are friends, you should find some nice stationery and write me a proper letter. These scribbles will not do, they are meant for the common masses.

A butterfly is banging on the windowpane in the corridor and I must now rise to let it out. If your next letter is not to hand with heartwarming promptness, I shall declare you unfit for human consumption and throw you to the lions.

Love.

I

PS: The sparrow wins. Imelda: nil, Sparrow: one.

In her letters to him, she called him Angel Ears.

'Why Angel Ears?' I asked her, in Ward 33 (Psychiatric), Sir J. J. Hospital.

She turned her cool green eyes on me and smiled. For a while, her fingers stopped playing with the worn-out sheet that was covering her.

'Haven't you noticed? His ears are the sweetest thing about him. They look like bits of bacon curled up from too much frying.'

I had never thought of my father's ears. But later that evening, as he stood in the kitchen and cooked for me and my sister, scraping at a fry-up of potatoes, I saw that his ears were indeed unusual. When was the first time that she noticed his ears? Was it part of her falling in love with him, or did it happen in the hypersensitive moments that follow? And when she called him by that name the first time, did he respond immediately? He probably did, without asking why. They could be like that together.

It intrigues me, love. Especially theirs, which seems to have been full of codes and rituals, almost all of them devised by her. She also called him Mambo, and Augie March, but almost never by his given name, Augustine.

He called her Imelda, which was her name, and, sometimes, Beloved.

She had another name for him: Limb of Satan. LOS. I asked her about that late one night, when the two of us were smoking together on the balcony of our small flat in a city of small flats. Behind us the one-bedroom-hall-kitchen, all 450 square feet of it, was quiet. In front of us, the side of a tenement rose like a cliff-face. Two trees were framed in between the buildings and in the foliage of one, a streetlight flickered erratically. She started laughing, a harsh scrape of sound that might belong in a brothel.

'Because he was always tempting me to sin,' she said.

'Who was?' Susan, my sister, was awake. She fitted herself into the balcony, waving a hand at the cloud of smoke we were producing.

'Your father.'

'It's not a sin if you're married, is it?'

'It's always a sin according to the Wholly Roaming Cat Licks.'

'That can't be true.'

'Can it not? I think you're only supposed to do it if you want babies. I wanted four but Hizzonner said, "Then you pay for the other two." That, as they say, was that. And I had to give the twenty-six others away.'

'What!' Susan and I looked at each other. Were there hordes of siblings we knew nothing about?

'I gave them straight out of my womb,' she explained. 'I could always tell when it had happened. I'd hear a click and I would know I was pregnant again, and I'd pray to Our Lady to take the poor wee thing and give it to someone else who wanted a child. Maybe one of those women who buy wax babies to offer the said Lady at Mahim.'

'So you'd have . . .' I ventured.

'Abortions? No, what do you take me for? I'd just climb down five stairs and jump six.'

'Jump down the stairs?'

'Six steps and land with a thump, six times, to shake those little mites from their moorings.'

She turned to Susan.

'But if *you* get knocked up, you come and tell me and I'll come with you to the doctor. We'll get you D'd and C'd before you can say Dick with a Thing and a Tongue.'

3

'What is deed and seed?'

'Dilation and curettage. I don't know what exactly it is but it sounds like they open you up and put a young priest in there. Anyway, only doctors do it. So when you're knocked up, you'll get a proper doctor to fiddle with your middle, you hear? No back-street abortions for you.'

'What about adoption?' Susan asked.

'What about it?'

'Mother Teresa came to college and –'

'She came to your college?'

'Yes.'

'You didn't tell me.'

'I didn't?'

'No. No one tells me anything. What did she say?'

'She said that if we got pregnant we should carry the child to term and give it to her.'

'She said that? Gosh.'

She frowned and was silent for a moment, considering this.

'I suppose it comes from not having lived in the world for hundreds of years. She's lived in a convent, it's not her fault. But still. Suppose I got pregnant today. Suppose I got nice and big and everyone asked, "When is it due?" and "My, you're carrying in the front, it must be a boy," and "What do you want? Pink or blue?" – and after all that, there's no baby at my breast. What do you think they'd think? What would I say? "Oh, I carried the baby to term and then I sent him off to Mother T because I couldn't afford him and I didn't want to have an abortion . . . ?"'

'Maybe you're supposed to hide,' I said.

'Oh yes, go away for a vacation for six or seven months. Where?'

'Goa?'

'Goa!' she said theatrically. 'That's worse than having it in Bombay. You might as well take an advert out in *O Heraldo* – "Fallen woman available for gawking and comments behind hankies. Holy Family parish church, Sunday Mass. For personal appointments and the full story, contact Father so and so." '

She shook her head.

'That's what comes of all this celibacy business. We confess to men who've never had to worry about a family. Naturally, it's a huge sin to them, this abortion business. What do *they* know? They probably think it's fun and games. Let them try it. I remember poor Gertie. Once, she was sure that it had happened –'

'An abortion?'

'No, stupid, a pregnancy – she was late, and she was *never* late, so she knew. She took me out after work and we stood on the street near Chowpatty beach and she ate three platefuls of papaya. I thought she was constipated. But then we went to Bombelli's and she had three gins as if they were cough syrup. That was when she told me what she was trying to do. "Bake the poor thing out of there," she said. "It gets too hot inside, the bag squeezes and the baby pops out. I hope." She came to the office the next day and she looked like death warmed over. Apparently, it had worked. "Baby, if something like that happens to you, you go and get it D'd and C'd. It's not worth it," she said to me. And now I say unto you, Sue, and to you too . . .' she said, looking at me.

'Me?'

'Yes, you. Not that you're going to get pregnant any which way you turn out. But if you do put a loaf in some poor

5

girl's oven, you will take her to a government place, you will announce that you are Mr and Mrs D'Souza –'

'Why D'Souza?'

'I don't know. Some name. Any name. Not hers. And after it's done you will take her somewhere to rest and relax and weep and you will stay with her until she can go home.'

'You mean I'm not to tell her to jump down six stairs and give the baby to Our Lady?'

'You are a wicked young man to laugh at an old lady's guilt,' said Em. But she was smiling too.

She was always Em to us. There may have been a time when we called her something ordinary like Mummy, or Ma, but I don't remember. She was Em, and our father, sometimes, was The Big Hoom. Neither Susan nor I, the only persons who might ever care to investigate the matter, can decide how those names came about, though we've tried ('Em must mean M for Mother' and 'Maybe it's because he made "hoom" sounds when we asked him something'). On certain days we called her Doogles, or The Horse, or other such names that sprang from some subterranean source and vanished equally quickly. Otherwise, she was Em, and most of the time she was Em with an exclamation mark.

Once, by mistake, I called her Mater. I got it out of a Richie Rich comic. The very rich, very snobby Mayda Munny used the word to address her mother. I should have known that I would not get away with something so precious, but I was nine or ten years old and did not know what precious meant. Em peered at me for a moment, pulling deeply on her beedi. (She smoked beedis because they were cheap, she said, and because once you'd started down the beedi road, you could never find your way back to the mild taste of cigarettes. The Big Hoom rarely came home from work in the evenings with sweets for us when we were children, but he never forgot the two bundles of Ganesh Chhaap Beedi.)

'Mater,' she said, and her eyes shone behind the curls of smoke. 'Yes, I suppose I am. I did do it, didn't I? And here you stand, living proof.'

I think I blushed. She roared, a happy manic laugh.

'I thought you boys knew everything about the cock and cunt business!'

'We do,' I said, lamely, terrified of where the conversation was going.

'So what did you think, both of you were products of the Immaculate Conception? Gosh, you couldn't keep us out of bed in those first years.'

'Em!'

'What? Are you feeling all Oedipal-Shmeedipal then?'

'What's Oedipal?'

Em loved a good story. She was off.

'Ick,' I said when Oedipus wandered off, his eyes bleeding and his future uncertain, escorted by his daughter who was also his sister.

'Well you may say "Ick",' said Em. 'But that's what Freud says every boy wants to do to his mother. Ick, I say to Mr Freud. He must have been odd, even for an Austrian. Not that I'm racist, but why would they have a navy when they're landlocked?'

'Mr Freud was in the navy?' I asked, confused.

'No, silly, I'm talking about *The Sound of Music*.'

The Big Hoom came into the bedroom.

'You're telling the boy about?'

'The psychoanalytic movement,' said Em, her voice slightly defiant.

'Have you got past the id, the ego and the superego?' he asked pleasantly.

'I should have started at that end, shouldn't I?'

'At what end did you start?'

'Oh, I was telling him about the Oedipus Complex.'

The Big Hoom said nothing. He did nothing. He looked at her. She went into a tizzy.

'It's knowledge, knowledge is good, it will help, knowledge *always* helps,' she said. She was attempting logic. But she was miserable. It was only later that I came to understand why she never used her condition as a refuge: it would have violated her sense of fair play. The Big Hoom let her stew for a bit and then he nodded. He opened *The Hamlyn Children's Encyclopaedia*, a book that I refused to read because it had been given to Susan as a birthday present, and slowly led me through the facts of life.

This might have been enough, but my mind was already locked on to what Em had told me. 'Why do boys want to do that with their mothers?' I asked.

A lesser man might have run shrieking from the question, or told his son to shut up. The Big Hoom taught me the word hypothesis, instead, and explained a little bit about Freud and tried to clear things up. Finally, he set me to making words out of 'hypothesis' and promised me ten paise for every word after the twentieth.

I loved the word hypothesis. It sounded adult and beautifully alien. I had never heard anything like it before. I wanted more words like it. I felt, instinctively, that when you had enough words like hypothesis, you would be able to deal with the world. I wasn't sure I would ever be able to deal with the world. It seemed too big and demanding and there wasn't a fixed syllabus.

I didn't know how to deal with what we were as a family, either. I didn't really know *what* we were as a family. I only knew that something was wrong with all of us and that it had something to do with my mother and her nerves.

'What are nerves?' I had asked The Big Hoom once. I didn't really want to know but a question was a good way to get him to pay attention to me. He put down his newspaper and took me into the gallery. Outside, wires snaked and writhed between the buildings of our housing colony. He pointed to them.

'What are those?'

I hated these moments. I wanted to be told, I did not want to be asked.

'Wires,' I said.

'What do wires do?'

'Electricity?'

'Yes, they carry electric current,' he said. 'Nerves do that inside the body.'

Thoughts, like electric currents, and inside my mother's head they ran uncontrolled – flashing and sizzling. I carried that image with me through my childhood for what ailed my mother and took her to hospital, sometimes every few months. Then she gave me another.

She was in Ward 33 again, lying in bed, a bed with a dark green sheet and a view of the outside. We could both see a man and a woman getting out of a taxi. They were young and stood for a while, as if hesitating, in front of the hospital. Then the man took the woman's hand in his and they walked into the hospital and we lost them.

'That's why Indian women fall ill,' Em said. 'So that their husbands will hold their hands.'

'Is that why you're here?'

I wanted to bite my tongue. I wanted to whiz around the world, my red cape flying, and turn time back so that I could choose not to make that remark. But Em, being Em, was already replying.

'I don't know, Baba, I don't know why. It's a tap somewhere. It opened when you were born.'

I was repaid in pain, a sharp thing.

'I loved you. And before you I loved Susan, the warmth of her and the smiles and the tiny toes and the miracle of her fingernails and the way her scrapes would fade within the day as she healed and grew. I loved the way her face lit up when she saw me and the way she nursed. But after you came along . . .'

She turned to the window again. An ambulance turned in, lazily, in the way of the city's ambulances. Inured to traffic, unconcerned by mortality, unimpressed by anyone's urgency, the ambulance driver stopped to light a beedi before jumping out of the cab. We watched together as someone inside opened the doors and two young men leapt out and tried to wrest a stretcher from within.

'Was it like that?' she asked. She had forgotten how she got to the hospital.

'No,' I said. 'You came in a taxi.'

'What was I wearing?'

'The green dress with the pockets.'

She looked puzzled.

I rooted about in the locker by the bed, a locker marked 'Patient Belonging', and opened it. I pulled the dress out.

'Oh that one,' she said. 'Bring it here.'

She stroked it as if to rediscover a little more about it.

'The tap?' I said.

'Sorry. I must be going mad.'

We both smiled at this, but only a little. It was a tradition: the joke, the smile.

'After you were born, someone turned on a tap. At first it was only a drip, a black drip, and I felt it as sadness. I had felt sad before . . . who hasn't? I knew what it was like. But I didn't know that it would come like that, for no reason. I lived with it for weeks.'

'Was there a drain?'

'No. There was no drain. There isn't one even now.'

She was quiet for a bit.

'It's like oil. Like molasses, slow at first. Then one morning I woke up and it was flowing free and fast. I thought I would drown in it. I thought it would drown little you, and Susan. So I got up and got dressed and went out onto the road and tried to jump in front of a bus. I thought it would be a final thing, quick, like a bang. Only, it wasn't.'

Her hands twitched at the sheet.

'I know.'

'Yes, the scar's still there.'

We were silent. I didn't want to hear this. I wanted to hear it.

'The bus stopped and the conductor had to take me to a hospital in a taxi. He sat in the front, lotus pose.'

'Lotus?'

'My blood was flowing across the floor of the taxi. There was no drain there either. I remember it all, as if rain had fallen. Have you ever noticed how rain clears the air? Everything stands out but it also looks a little thinner, as if the dust had been keeping things together. I felt as if . . .'

Her hands twitched at the sheet again. It slipped off her foot and both of us looked at the scar that ran from under the big toe to her ankle, a ridge of scar tissue.

'It had to be dressed every day for months. Dr Saha came and did the honours.'

'Don't wander,' I said.

'Where was I?'

'In the taxi. With the world outside clear.'

She looked a little confused.

'You said the world was clear.'

'Oh, not the world. Inside my head.'

Each time she had tried to kill herself she had opened her body and let her blood flow out. Was that the drain, then, I wondered, was that how it worked?

'And this time?' I asked her. 'Is it clear now?'

'This time I heard a small voice inside my head, just as I was beginning to slip away. I heard it say, "Please save me."'

'That was you.'

'No, I heard it.'

'It was you,' I said again.

'It must have been, no? I heard it as if it were someone else. And then you came. And Susan. I didn't want it that way. I didn't want the two of you to see anything like that in your lives.'

We had gone out together that afternoon, Susan and I, even though The Big Hoom was at work. It was a time of plenty. The stock market had worked in The Big Hoom's favour and he had sold some shares. A nurse had been hired and Em was, for once, someone else's responsibility.

We were teens on an adventure, watching *Coolie*, the biggest Amitabh Bachchan hit of 1983. The Big Hoom wouldn't have approved, and Em would have mocked, but they would never find out. We had laughed a lot, happy that we could go out and laugh, like all the others we knew who were our age. And it was a warm afternoon, the kind made for laughing. When the show was over and we came home, the nurse was asleep. She had no idea where Em was – this, in a house with a single bedroom, one living room, one small kitchen, two narrow corridors, one four-by-two balcony. Susan knew. She headed straight for the bathroom. There was no reply. She called, 'Em, Em,' panic streaking her voice. I knocked and called too. Finally, we heard something wet and slithery inside, and the door opened.

'I tried it again,' Em said. She was drenched in blood. It was in her hair. It was on her hands. It was dripping from her clothes.

I pulled out the immersion rod to warm some water. Susan went for the nurse, but she, wily lady, had taken one look over our shoulders and vanished into the still-warm afternoon. Susan called The Big Hoom. I heard her in some other way, not the normal way you hear things. It was thin and distant but it was also clear. I can still hear it if I try. I don't. Em was leaning against the wall next to the bathroom door and shivering. I guided her to the low metal stool and she sat down. Her arms dangled between her knees. I picked up one of her arms and turned it over to look. The cut was a single line, dark red. It said nothing.

'Em tried to kill herself,' I heard Susan say.

Then she was back.

'What did he say?' I asked.

'What do you think?' she was impatient as she tested the water with her finger. 'He says he's coming.'

I poured warm water over Em, from her head downwards. The water ran red. Susan reached down in front of Em and began to raise her dress and petticoat. I excused myself. My mother was going to be stripped naked.

I went out and made the next call. To Granny, Em's mother, solid woman, cloth and sawdust solid.

'Coming,' said Granny.

'Take a taxi,' I said.

'Taking,' said Granny.

I stood in the balcony for a while. The traffic flowed outside. A sparrow dropped onto the balcony. A crow followed. The sparrow fluttered away. The crow preened cockily. A chickoo seller announced that his wares came from Gholvad. Then I went to make tea with lots of sugar. I had read somewhere that sugar helps with shock. Who was shocked?

When Em and Susan came out, I brought them tea. Susan sat Em down and held the tea cup to her lips. I went into the bathroom and turned on all the taps. I let the water flood out onto the floor. The stick broom, which had a tendency to fall on its side after it was used, was saturated in blood. There were clots that looked like hairballs – I still don't know what they were – and they kept clogging the drain. I gathered them with my foot in one corner where they could not impede the flow of the water, the draining of the blood. I smelt the odour that trains leave on your fingers: iron. In some odd part of my brain, something about the link between iron and anaemia and haemoglobin and blood clicked into place. I went down and bought a bottle of iron tonic.

When I returned, Granny and The Big Hoom had arrived. He was already in the bathroom, cleaning up. Granny was in the bedroom, talking to Em and drinking tea.

I don't remember what we did that evening. I don't remember going to sleep or waking up the next morning. I only remember the moment Dr Saha, the family GP, came. He clicked his tongue and bandaged Em – her wrists this time. The Big Hoom was not a fan of bandages; he believed that sunlight and air did more good if you kept things clean, but he didn't object.

'Should she go to the hospital?' he asked.

'See how she sleeps,' Dr Saha said.

We slept that night, so Granny and The Big Hoom must have kept watch over Em. And something must have changed in the night because she was not there the next morning. We began our hospital visits: one day Susan, one day me, every day The Big Hoom. On one of these visits, she told me about the tap that opened at my birth and the black drip filling her up and it tore a hole in my heart. If that was what she could manage with a single sentence, what did thirty years of marriage do to The Big Hoom?

2.

'Hello, buttercup'

Imelda saw Augustine in the office. Her diary reads:

I finally located the source of the booming voice. I asked
Andrade, who is the registered office flirt, about the noise
and he said, 'Oh, that's AGM.' I looked a bit puzzled and he
looked a bit puzzled. 'I don't know his name. We all call him
AGM. His initials, I think.'

'Don't you like him?' I asked.

'Oh, he's a great guy. You'll see.'

'And you don't know his name?'

'I do. It's AGM,' he said.

Now what do you say to that?

I think I might like it here, as long as they don't give me
too many numbers to type . . .

We had carte blanche to read Em's diaries and letters.
Sometimes she read them out to us, her spectacles perched
high on her nose, the black frame hiding her thick eyebrows.
I never saw her tear up anything; every scrap and note written to her went into a series of cheerful cloth bags. On
certain days, she would rummage around in the bags and
pull out a note, a fragment, a whole letter. She would glance
at some, read some in full, and dream.

While Em's letters were public documents in the family, neither Susan nor I read her diaries during her lifetime (Susan still won't). Perhaps we had understood very early that they would give us no clues to her illness, or ways to reach her on her worst days. Or – and this may be closer to the truth – we were afraid of what we might find there, and afraid of having to deal with it. Even now, I look in Em's notebooks not for my mother but for Augustine's Beloved.

It didn't take Augustine, aka AGM, long to spot the new girl in the office of ASL – Ampersand Smith Limited – the engineering goods company at which Imelda was the new stenotypist and he was the junior manager, sales. Two days later, he spoke to her:

> Booming Voice spoke to me. What nerve. He bounces past my desk, flashes his blue peepers at me and says, 'Hello buttercup,' and ricochets off the opposite wall to do something else.

I find it difficult to picture my father in these entries. To me, he seemed built for endurance, not speed. The thought of him ricocheting off walls is odd. I have tried reconstructing him in my head, dressing him in what up-and-coming young men wore to the office at the time: white shirt, black trousers, black shoes and socks. Like all such men, he probably also kept another couple of shirts with him, and a tin of talcum powder, so that he could change when the humidity leached his shirt of its starch. He was a man who liked women. When he won *The Illustrated Weekly of India*'s crossword contest, he bought every woman in his office a yellow rose with a little fern wrapped in white tissue and tied with a yellow satin ribbon. For that day, so Gertrude told Imelda, the office had felt like a garden. And for weeks the perfume of the roses had lingered, if not in reality, then at least in the imaginations of the young women of ASL. Gertrude had opened her bag and showed Imelda that the satin ribbon still lay at the bottom.

'To remind me that all men aren't the same, dear,' she had said. Gertrude was a veteran of the love wars. She had been 'carrying on' with a married man for so many years, she had lost count. 'And to add insult to injury, dear, he's Muzzlim.'

Imelda was too young to understand that love could be an injury. She was too young to understand why Motasim's religion was an added insult.

She was also too young to respond to 'Hello buttercup'. So she hadn't.

'Why didn't you?' Gertrude was surprised.

'I didn't know what to say.'

'You could have said "Hello"?'

But in all the films Imelda had seen, the suave young man would say 'Hello buttercup' and the heroine would answer such impudence with the kind of remark that would stop his airy advance through fields of irises and daisies and tansies. Such a crisp response marked her as someone different from the rest, a fitting sparring partner, someone to love.

That day, 'Hello, buttercup' had seemed unanswerable, and Imelda had only managed a weak roll of the eyes – 'not even with the panache of Anna Magnani,' she recalled. Gertrude did not know all this. In her world, men went hunting and women waited to be hunted. But when a man began to circle, it was up to the prey to draw the hunter in.

'Unless you're a fool for love, my dear,' she said, over

a Coke float at Bombelli's. 'Unless you throw your cap over a windmill.'

Gertrude became Imelda's closest friend at ASL, and would have been her guide in matters of the heart, had her own love life not been so pitted with compromise. At first, Gertrude's allusions to her secret sorrow over Motasim caused Imelda deep distress. But over a couple of weeks she began to see that the references were mechanical. Gertrude had settled into a comfortable pattern in which she had love and tragedy in equal measure, and a male presence in her life to warm her bed and take her to dak bungalows in hill stations, but never to get in the way of her decisions.

'Buy your own house, I say to all the girls. I can see them thinking, "Who's this soiled dove to give us advice?" But my heart is good and I know what's what and God is my judge. If it's your home, you can do what you want there. If it's your home, no one is going to tell you to sit if you want to stand.'

'Not even Motasim, Gertie?' asked Imelda.

'*Certainly* not Motasim,' said Gertrude. 'Do you know he wasn't married when we met? And it was like that –' and here she snapped her fingers.

'*Un coup de foudre!*' said Imelda happily. She had always wanted one of those to happen, not necessarily to her but to someone, so she could watch from a safe distance.

'That only. He took one look at me at Andrade's – this was after the flickers, we had all gone from the office – *one* look and he knew. He was looking at me, saying with his eyes, "I want, I want." I was so young then, so innocent. I believed in love.'

Like many women Gertrude saw herself as a cynic, largely because the man she loved would not marry her and because she had two cigarette holders – one of onyx and one of mother-of-pearl – which she dug out of her capacious bag when she could be bothered. And finally, because there had once been a good young man, a medical representative, who had loved her and wanted to take her away from it all.

'And so I put in a word,' she told me on one of the few occasions she came to meet her old, old friend Imelda, our Em. She chose her times carefully, never coming when Em wanted to meet her. She would come when Em was depressed and withdrawn. This meant Susan or I had to entertain her for the mandatory forty-five minutes which she thought constituted a visit to a sick friend. Then she could go away and pretend to be offended when Em really did want to see her. I could see that she thought this made her a friend in need. It was one of my first lessons in the self-deception people practise on themselves. I hated talking to Gertrude for this reason. But I loved talking to her because she had known Em when she was whole. I loved it also because talking to anyone normal was an invitation to the world of ordinary people who had ordinary woes and wor-ries: money, sex, sin and real estate, for instance. They were not, or so I imagined, people with ambivalences about their mothers or fears about their own acceptability.

'I put in a word with your father,' Gertrude said. 'If you're looking to talk to her, I told him, you'll have to go a little easy. No yorricking about.'

'Yorricking?'

'You'll have to step carefully, I told him. She wasn't like one of us; she wouldn't love'em and leave'em. And she seemed lost, I could tell.'

*

Gertrude was right. Em was not quite sure what she was doing in an office. She began her day with Mass; or she was supposed to. And then she was on the tram to work. It seemed like a job she could have done in her sleep: taking dictation and typing letters, doing the filing and answering telephones. Em had been a teacher before this, and I could imagine her as one. I couldn't see her as a steno. My version of elitism, perhaps.

'The job was all right, but I was a little worried about being in a big office with adults,' she told us.

'Adults? Weren't you one?'

'Technically, I was. But I didn't think of myself that way. All those cartoons about "Come in and take some dictation" and being chased around the desk . . . and I hadn't even *wanted* to be an office girl.'

When Em finished her Senior Cambridge at the age of sixteen, she had thought she was going to college. She dreamt of standing at the bus stop, chattering with her friends and refusing to admit that those boys were looking. She dreamt of lectures and Milton and prosody ('It sounded so naughty'). She dreamt of French literature. In the confines of her head, she debated whether she would wear dresses like the other Roman Catholic and Anglo-Indian girls of Byculla or whether she would follow the Coelho sisters in their khadi saris and Kolhapuri chappals – carelessly, gorgeously beautiful, incidental flowers in their hair.

She stopped dreaming when she came home with her certificate and the good wishes of her teachers.

'Daddy will ask,' Granny said. 'You say no.'

Em's mother spoke in code. She omitted almost all the important words in every sentence. She had had far too many languages drummed into her ears – first Konkani in Goa, then Burmese in Rangoon, then Bengali in wartime Calcutta, and now English, in which her child spoke and dreamed. It had taken away most of her vocabulary. She communicated through gestures, facial expressions and the assumption that everyone knew what she was talking about. It doesn't sound likely, but it worked.

Em realized that she was being asked to say that she had no wish to go to college. She didn't understand why. So Granny told her.

'Where there is? You have to. I can't. How long?'

Em understood. There was no money for college. She would have to work. Granny had scrounged and saved for too long on granddad's modest salary – a mathematics teacher's salary. Besides, college would take an awful lot of time.

'She was right. Daddy did ask if I wanted to go to college,' Em said. 'I couldn't say "No" because I wanted to go and I didn't want to lie. I asked, "Where will the money come from?" I was hoping he would have an answer. A gold wristwatch that he could sell, a ruby he had smuggled in from Burma. Anything. But he only said, "That can be arranged." And I knew it would mean taking a loan and maybe the house would go. I didn't talk about it again, and he didn't talk about it either.'

Instead Granny went out looking and found her a job at a school run by nuns.

'They hired you?' I asked.

'How could they? I was sixteen. So the nuns told Ma they would hire Astrid instead. Astrid the Ostrich, you know?'

'No. I don't.'

'You don't remember Astrid the Ostrich? No, she must

have been before your time. Astrid DeSa, poor dear, she's dead. Died not long after she replaced me at the school – that's what I heard. She was at the blackboard and she put her hand up to her head and coughed once. Then she threw up her lunch, right on the blackboard, and slumped. The stain is still there, they say. By the time the other teachers came, she was gone.'

'She died with her boots on.'

'That's supposed to mean you died happy. Did she? I don't know. Who can know? I would like to die with my boots on too. But what would that mean? I haven't had any boots for a while. I don't know that I ever had boots. I think I had booties once – booties . . . sounds like something you develop if you don't wash. Or is that cooties? Spellings! I could never bear American spelling, not even when I took their dollars. For me, it was always the Queen's English. How I longed to type "colour" at the AmConGen . . . that's the American Consulate, before you ask.'

We didn't have to ask. We knew that she worked there, after leaving ASL.

'Why couldn't you type it?'

'Type what?'

'Colour.'

'I could type. No, I meant I couldn't type it with a "u". I had to do it all without "u". And then *you* came along. Gosh. That's another story.'

Conversations with Em could be like wandering in a town you had never seen before, where every path you took might change course midway and take you with it. You had to keep finding your way back to the main street in order to get anywhere.

'So what did Astrid DeSa have to do with your job?' I asked.

'Oh, she had the paperwork. She had a Teacher's Certificate. But she couldn't work because she had had twins and there were abscesses on her nipples and she always said, "My boys drink my milk and pus and blood." In my head, I called one Pus and the other Blood for a long time . . . So the nuns hired her on paper but I did the teaching.'

'And Astrid agreed?'

'She got twenty per cent.'

'Of your salary?'

'Of my salary. I got sixty per cent.'

'And the rest?'

'A donation to the work of Jesus.'

'It went to the nuns?'

'Don't be harsh. They did all this to help your Granny. They could easily have turned her away.'

'And you could have gone to college.'

'Could I?' She frowned. 'I suppose I could have. But I would have had to ask Daddy. And he would have had to take a loan. And the house would have gone.'

'Really? To send just one student to college?'

I tried to believe Em in everything she said. It was my act of faith, because I could see how the outside world immediately discounted whatever she said. But I wanted so hard to believe that I often found myself in the position of the inquisitor, the interrogator, demanding verification, corroboration, further proof. Most of the time, she didn't seem to mind.

'I know. It seems odd. It's cheap now, so says Angel Ears. I thought we would have a tough time when Sue started college. I said he and I could eat bread and drink water and he laughed and said, "No. It's not a problem, the fees are not a problem."'

Then she was wandering again.

'You know, I thought he was being all big and manly about it, sending his little girl to college, because the students had gone on strike and tried to set fire to a bus. Only the poor dears didn't quite manage to; the papers showed the bus the next morning and it looked quite all right except the stuffing on the seats was torn. I think they should have got some expert advice from Calcutta. They burn buses there, don't they?'

'Em. We were talking about your going to college.'

'Oh, I couldn't. Not now. I've read those nice *Reader's Digest* things where an old lady goes to college and everyone is fond of her, but I don't think it would be the same. I don't want to study now. And I don't want people to be fond of me. It sounds like I'd be the sheepdog of the class. Or I'd have to be a muddha-figure and for that I've got the two of you and God knows I messed that up as well.'

'Oh come on.'

'That's sweet of you. But see, if you weren't a messed up child, *my* messed up child, you would have made a nice long speech about how I was the perfect mother. But you can't. So we're all messed up by *Reader's Digest* standards. We'll never make it to a heart-rending story you can read on your summer vacation.'

'Em, you're not listening. Was college really that expensive in your time?'

'I don't know. I don't know what it cost . . . How old are you?'

'Shouldn't you know?'

'Shouldn't you?'

'Seventeen.'

'Gosh, seventeen and so many questions! I couldn't ask questions like that. I didn't say: show me the bank books. But I knew I had to bring in some money. So I put on my blue dress with the lace collar and went to work.'

Em would tell us that she liked being a schoolteacher, and from memories I have of Em combing a young patient's hair in her hospital ward, or feeding the old lady in the bed next to hers as she would feed an infant, I can believe this. But her first day as a teacher nearly destroyed her. Schoolchildren can smell a nervous teacher. They see it in her gait as she enters the room, uncertain of her ability to command and instruct. They hear it in her voice as she clears her throat before she begins to speak. They sense it when she looks at the teacher's table and chair, set on a platform to give her a view of the class, as if she has no right to be there. They watch without remorse or sympathy as she walks the gauntlet and suddenly they are in the grip of a completely new sensation. It is power that they are feeling as they anneal into a single organism: the class. At any moment now, they will cry havoc and let slip the dogs of war. Every schoolchild has felt that collective rill of joy trickle down his throat as the hierarchy breaks down and revenge may be had.

'I think Mother Superior meant well,' Em remembered. 'But she made a fatal mistake. She came and introduced me and said that I was the new teacher and that it was my first day at teaching. She said she knew what well-behaved children they were and how they would help me. For a few minutes after she left, they tolerated me. Or they held themselves back. I remember trying to think what teachers did or said. No one had even told me what I was supposed to be teaching. I asked what period it was and the class shouted back in one voice, "Mathematics." I almost wept, because I *hated* mathematics and now it seemed I was supposed to be teaching it. In the next five minutes, they were ready. All of them had pieces of paper under their feet. They began rubbing them on the floor. Khuzzz. Khuzzz. Khuzzz. I said, "Please don't do that," or something. I knew it wasn't the right thing to say. I knew I sounded weedy. But that was all I could manage.'

'Gosh,' I said, feeling a pang of guilt. The future sins of the son had been visited on the mother. How many times had I helped do this to a new teacher?

'They all chorused, "So-rry tea-cher." I said, "That's all right." They chorused, "Than-kyou tea-cher . . ." I can still hear their voices, the dirty little shits, though I came to love them later, but they were still dirty little shits . . . and then they began singing "Happy birthday" to me.'

'What did you do?'

'I ran out of the class crying.'

'What?'

'I was terrified. I just wanted to hide somewhere so I thought I'd hide in a toilet. Only, it was the boys' toilet.'

'Oh God.'

'Luckily, it was empty. Then I found the staffroom by mistake and Mother Superior was there, examining workbooks or something. She made me wash my face and then she took me back to class. She made the class kneel down on their desks and pray for forgiveness to the benevolent God who had allowed them to be born in families that sent them to school.'

'The Hindus and Muslims too?'

'Everyone. Then they had to write a letter of apology to their parents. She was quite, quite brilliant, Mother Soup.'

'Who were you teaching?'

'Seventh standard. I think she assumed I couldn't do too much damage there. I must have been a terrible teacher because I didn't understand any of the stuff I was teaching. Each day I'd ask Daddy what to say about integers or fractions or ratio and proportion and I would read it out slowly in class. Then I would make a clever boy come up to the blackboard and do the sums.'

'Wow,' I said.

'What does that mean? No, don't bother telling me. As if I don't know. But what could I do? I didn't understand ratio and proportion. The numbers seemed to skip about, some went up and some went down and nothing seemed to work out. But after a year, they gave me English and history. I was so happy I could have danced.'

But at the end of six months, Granny arrived in Mother Soup's office. Her daughter was now eighteen years old and she was no longer going to work at the school. She wouldn't teach anymore, but learn. She would join the Standard Shorthand and Typewriting Institute.

' "We set the standard", that was their motto. Mae said it was the right thing for me to do. Someone must have told her that secretaries make more money. Or something like that. So she decided that I would become a secretary.'

'Did she ask you?'

Em gave me a speaking look.

28

'I was so unhappy I wept almost all the time. I remember a couple of my students passing me on the street and saying, "Good morning, Miss" and I burst into tears. I remember crying because I didn't think I would ever be able to change a typewriter ribbon without getting my fingers dirty. I remember crying because I didn't understand tabs. And just when I had started to understand the typing thing, the shorthand started and the typing seemed like easy butter-jelly-jam. Typing was about getting English out of a machine. Shorthand was a new language and it was terrible, full of chays and jays and things like that. I can't tell you how much I cried.'

How to read those tears would always be a problem. For anyone else, they would be the outpourings of an eighteen-year-old forced out of a world she had grown to enjoy into a new one. But each time Em told me something about her life, I would examine it for signs, for early indications of the 'nervous breakdown'. It was an obsession and might have something to do with my curiosity about her life. She was born in Rangoon, I knew, and had come to India on one of the ships that crossed the Bay of Bengal when the Japanese attacked Burma. Her father had walked, from Rangoon to Assam; legend has it that he had departed with a head of black hair and appeared again in Calcutta with a shock of white hair. Was this it? Was this the break? She didn't seem to remember much about that crossing except how she used orange sweets to quell her nausea and began menstruating on board the ship. Was this just how people remembered things, in patches and images, or was this the repression of a painful memory?

Somewhere along the way their piano had been jettisoned

to lighten the boat. When I first heard this, I thought it was a good place for things to start, for my mother's breakdown to begin. I imagined the dabbassh as the piano hit the water with, perhaps, a wail of notes. I imagined my mother weeping for the piano as it began to bubble its way to the bottom of the Bay of Bengal. I cut between her tears, the white handkerchief handed to her by her impatient mother, the plume of dust rising from the seabed, the tear-soaked face, the first curious fish . . .

Then I heard another Roman Catholic Goan family speak of their piano. And another. And a fourth. Then I got it. The pianos were a metaphor, a tribal way of expressing loss. It did not matter if the pianos were real or had never existed. The story was their farewell to Rangoon. It expressed, also, their sense of being exiled home to Goa, to a poor present. The past could be reinvented. It could be rich with Burmese silk and coal mines and rubies and emeralds and jade. It could be filled with anything you wanted and a piano that was thrown overboard could express so much more than talking about how one lent money out at interest in the city. Or how one taught English to fill up the gaps of a schoolteacher's salary.

The family had come to Goa and then to Bombay. They had lived in a single room that would later become a laundry before Em's father found a job as a mathematics teacher. Was that it? The years of deprivation? Only, it didn't seem to be much more deprivation than many young women of the time endured. Was it the sacrifice of her teaching job, then? Hundreds of women had sacrificed the same or more. Every fact, every bit of information had to be scanned. Sometimes it was exhausting to listen to her because she seemed to be throwing out clues faster than I could absorb them.

Eventually Em did learn to type sixty words per minute and take dictation. The Standard Shorthand and Typewriting Institute awarded her a certificate and gave her a special mention for her shorthand.

'Which is very good, even if I say so myself. Most of the other girls couldn't read their own shorthand one hour later. I can still read my notes thirty years after I made them.'

For the next two months, Em worked with a small firm called Mehta Mechanical Electrical and Engineering Corporation.

'It was called Memecorp. So Baig the joker called it Mommecorp.'

'Didn't get that one.'

'He spoke some Konkani.'

'Oh right. Sorry.'

Momme, in demotic Konkani, is the word for breasts.

Despite its rather grand name, Memecorp was not a particularly good place to work.

'They paid me a daily wage. If I went in, I got paid. If I didn't, I didn't. And two or three times, I went in and they said there's no work for you today so you can go and I had to go, even though I had paid my tram fare.'

'Like a labourer.'

'That's what I thought. So I kept an eye out, and one day I saw an ad for a steno in ASL and I applied. There was an Anglo-Indian lady at the reception desk. She looked at me and said, "Have you been teaching, dearie?" I said, "Yes." She smiled at me and said, "It shows." I was such a duffer then,

I didn't even know that she was insulting me. I said, "Yes, I want to go back and teach but we need the money at home." She said, "My, you won't get a job as a steno if you look like a teacher, dearie." Then she gave me a card and told me to go and see a certain gentleman. "He'll kit you out in the latest style," she said. "What about the job interview?" I asked. "You won't get the job," she said. "Go on now." That's when I got a bit angry and said, "I'd like to take my chances." I sat down and waited.'

'And you got the job?'

Then, as now, I loved a happy ending. And at least this little bit of Em's story had a happy ending.

'Of course I did,' she snorted. 'I wrote good English and I knew when to use a dictionary. I knew grammar. They gave me a little test and I think I did very well on it. They also asked me to draft a letter to the bank asking for an overdraft. I didn't know what an overdraft was so I kept it simple. But, as Andrade told me later, that was what got me the job.'

At the end of the test and a short interview, Em left but found the receptionist missing. She was having a cigarette outside the building, oblivious to the men staring at her.

'I felt a bit triumphant as I told her that I had been offered the job. "Are you taking it?" she asked. I thought she must be out of her mind. In those days jobs were scarce and you took what you were offered. But she asked again, "Are you taking it?" I thought perhaps she had a sister and her sister had her eye on the job, so I said, "Yes. And I told them so." Then I thought I would be kind and I said, "But I'll need some new clothes so I'll go to that gentleman who you said will kit me out." But she didn't seem very happy with that. She started saying that it wasn't a good idea, I already had the job, so why bother? I don't know why but I became stubborn. "I don't want to look like a teacher," I said. "What's wrong with being a teacher?" she asked. "Nothing," I said, "but I'm a steno in a big firm now so I want to look like that." I don't know why I was saying these things. I thought my clothes were all right, but there was something about Brigitte that made me say these things. I think she oozed a challenge. Do you remember that film we saw about the Bengali woman taking up a job?'

'*Mahanagar*?'

We'd seen it together for some reason. It must have been on the Saturday evening slot that was reserved for 'regional cinema' on Doordarshan. We couldn't have gone to a neighbour's house to watch it. Not with Em. So it would have been after we got our own television. The memory makes me smile: Em, with her beedi, and Susan and I watching Satyajit Ray on a Saturday evening, with The Big Hoom working overtime or busy in the kitchen. Even when we were a family, we weren't quite the usual.

'Is that the one?' Em asked. 'The one in which you thought the Anglo-Indian woman was a bad actress?'

'That's the one.'

'Brigitte was a little like her. She was the kind of girl who thought only she had the right to wear lipstick. She was the kind who would laugh at anyone who tried out a new fashion before she did. I hadn't even known her ten minutes but I knew the kind. So I thought she would be happy that I was taking some fashion advice from her. But she grabbed my arm and snarled at me. "What's your game then, you bitch?" I was so startled I could hardly speak. "Give me back that card," she said and her voice was like lava. And ice. Cold and angry. And her eyes were so full of hate, I flinched. I opened my handbag and began to rummage in it, frantically. Just then Andrade walked past and said, "Getting friendly, girls?" She let go of my arm and I rushed off. When I got home, my hands were still shaking. Mae looked at my face and said, "Never mind, you'll get the next one. I'm sure of it." She thought I hadn't got the job. She thought I'd made a mess of the interview. How could I tell her that I had been terrified by a receptionist?'

'Did you miss teaching?' Susan asked.

'No, actually, it was a big relief.'

I raised my eyebrows.

'You know, an office job means you don't have to carry anything home. Not if you're a steno, anyway. You do your work and you leave. Then you can forget about everything. You don't have to worry about Celestine's father who's a violent drunk and won't let him study. You don't have to bother about Fatima who's been taken out of school and her mother tells you she's too sickly to study and you know it's because they've arranged her marriage. No corrections. No papers to set. No destinies in your hands. Just some letters to type and some spellings to learn.'

'Spellings?'

'Machine names. They made electrostatic precipitators. I didn't even know whether they actually made the damned things or bought them from someone else. Don't look like that.'

'Like what?' I asked.

'You have your worst baby-Marxist look on your face.'

I had decided I was a socialist. One afternoon, the year before, I'd joined a protest march by mill workers that went

34

past our school. I'd walked among them for fifteen minutes raising slogans and feeling light-headed, and when I came back home, I'd let Em and Susan know. I was proud of my achievement. Em had laughed. 'Rite of passage. Next, you lose your virginity – and what a relief *that* will be.'

'I have no such look,' I said to her. 'You were telling me about electrostatic precipitators.'

'You do. You look like someone who's thinking, "My mother was part of the alienated workforce and she didn't mind it." Well, you shame me not. I was happy to type and take messages and eat my sandwiches and go for a movie on Saturdays. I didn't care whether the company made a profit or loss. I didn't care because my bonus came anyway and I got my salary anyway and I handed it over to Mae.'

'And thus you were alienated from your labour as well as from your wages.'

'I don't know about that. I lived the good life in my mother's house. I don't think I ever worried about how food was coming to the table or what was to be cooked. It appeared and I cribbed and I ate it and the plates went away again to be washed. I had no hand in any of that.'

'As the wage earner?'

Em looked a bit thoughtful.

'Oh, was that it? I thought it was just Mae's way.'

'Maybe it was. After all, other women earn but they also do the housework.'

'I think there was a time when she tried to teach me to cook. We were in Goa then. Some small fish had been brought from the river and there were still a few that were hopping about a bit. I couldn't bear it so I thought I'd drown them and put them out of their misery.'

'That sounds like an apocryphal family story.'

'It does? I thought it sounded like a really silly one. But if you know a word like apocryphal you should of course find a reason to trot it out. And there's a sequel. When Mae came in, she was horrified to find a couple of fish now swimming about so she took them down to the river and let them go again. So there.'

The wage earner was spared the housework. But this was how the money was apportioned: Imelda earned it and Mae doled out a weekly allowance.

'Sometimes I'd save my tram fare home. It was about an hour from Fort to Byculla if I walked, so I walked and saved my pence . . .'

'To eat dates,' I said.

'Yes. Dates. Clever of you to remember. Is there a fruit anywhere in the world like the date? I mean, have you ever met a disappointing date? I've met apples that do not crunch and I've met pears that are too hard. I've met grapes that are sour . . .'

'Okay, but a date is always sweet. I got that.'

'What would I do without you to keep me on the conversational straight and narrow?' Em waved her beedi in the air with a rhetorical flourish. 'I bought dates and I ate them as I walked.'

'It must have helped you stay slim.'

'You know, perhaps it was because there was so little money in the house, but I don't remember ever being worried about my figure. I knew it was okay and my face was okay and that was it. So I didn't think . . . no . . . I never thought: is this good for my figure? I never thought about that. And if someone had come up to me and offered me a lift home in his car, I would have hopped in. But only with someone respectable. We were always being told about horrible things happening to young women who got into cars with the wrong people. But no wrong people were to hand, thankfully, so there I was walking down the road from Fort to Bicks, eating a handful of dates, very slowly and very slyly, because I think it was generally felt that a woman should not eat in public.'

And one day, a car did pull up next to her.

3.

'If he should try and rape you'

'It was your Big Hoom, our very own LOS. He opened the door for me, but before I could get in, three young ladies from the bus stop rushed past me and got in. So he did the only thing a fellow could do.'

She stopped and looked at me expectantly.

'Which was?'

'He got out.'

'That must have pleased the taxi driver.'

'He was squawking but your Big Hoom didn't care much. He said, "Are you walking home?" "Yes," I said. "Well, I'll walk with you then." And we began to walk.'

'What happened to the taxi?'

'You're getting obsessed with that taxi. But it was strange. We went into a bookshop because he wanted to check if a book he had ordered had come. When we came out, it was waiting for us.'

'The same taxi?!'

'LOS had an arrangement with a driver. Something that he'd worked out so it benefited both of them. I never did figure it out but there was always a taxi and it was always the same driver.'

'And what happened to the women who got into the taxi? The ones from the bus stop?'

'Your father sold them into the flesh trade. I have no idea. I suppose they got out when they figured there was going to be no free ride. Why do you want to know?'

I had no idea why. I still don't. I like details – no, it's more than that; I delight in details. I'm never sure where I am with people who may give me the large truths about themselves but not the everyday, even trivial details – the book a friend was reading in the airplane on the way to Chicago, the number of times someone sat for his degree examination, the names of the dogs a friend had when he lived with his grandfather. I've been told that I exhaust people with my curiosity. Once I was told that living with me would mean being trapped and slowly asphyxiated. Should I blame Em for this? Or would I have turned out just the way I am even if she had been whole and it had been possible to reach her?

There's that bookshop, for instance. Em never told me the name, she couldn't remember, and I'm still trying to find out.

Because that was also part of the family legend. That Augustine and Imelda spent their courtship in a variety of bookshops, that they would still have been doing that if they'd had their own way. I told The Big Hoom about this view of the two of them and he looked amused for a moment and then annoyed for a moment.

'It wasn't like that,' he said and there was something in his voice that suggested it could never be like that. But he didn't tell me how it was exactly. He never said anything to contradict the view that neither of them seemed to want to get married; that they were content merely courting, like romantic adolescents unwilling to risk consummation.

He did tell me, though, about the time he first saw Em.

'I saw her at the office. She was very frightened. I don't think she was very much more than eighteen years old when she came to work at ASL. And then she had to deal with Brigitte.'

I'd wondered about Brigitte ever since Em told me of her interview at ASL.

'We knew there was something wrong,' The Big Hoom told me. 'But no one could say what it was. We found out only later when the police came to take her. I don't remember exactly how the racket worked, but those were days of terrible unemployment. Young women, quite respectable, would come to the office asking for jobs. Brigitte would send them off to a brothel somewhere.'

So that was why Em was being sent to the dressmaker. And why Brigitte was so reluctant to give her the address later. I made a mental note to tell Em about it some time. I knew it would make her happy, to find out why. Perhaps because I always thought of her as a writer who would like her stories shaped well.

There were notebooks all over the house, stacks of them. There was writing in odd places. And books were often annotated. Our clothbound copy of *The Collected Works of Lewis Carroll*, with illustrations by John Tenniel, was filled with scribbles. I still have that book. Chapter Three of *Through the Looking Glass* – 'Looking-Glass Insects' – has this scrawled over the title: 'To be or not to be, that is the question. Ha ha. I'm a humorist'. On the page where the guard is peering in at Alice and the goat through a pair of binoculars, is an inscription: 'Horrible illustrations! I'm frightened. Help me God!' The rather cheerful poem – cheerful for Carroll, at least – 'The Walrus and The Carpenter' has 'Ave Maria' written after every third verse.

This we knew about her even when everything else was a mystery: Em wrote. She wrote when she was with us. She wrote when no one was around. She wrote postcards, she wrote letters in books, she wrote in other people's diaries, in telephone diaries, on the menus of takeaway places. Did she really want to be a teacher? I ask myself now. Or did she want to be a writer? In some of the letters she wrote Augustine, she was obviously flaunting her ability to write. She was demonstrating her charm, her effortlessness, her skill. She was suggesting to the world that she be taken seriously as a writer. No one did. I didn't. I didn't even see it. I thought she wrote as she broadcast, without much effort, without much thought. I have discovered since that such effortlessness is not easy to achieve and its weightlessness is in direct proportion to the effort put in. But unless she wrote drafts in secret and destroyed them, she seems to have achieved lift-off without effort. And then there was no reason for her to work at it, really. She had no audience other than us.

Why didn't we see her as a writer? Her parents had an excuse; they needed money. Why didn't we?

But then there's equally this: How could we have seen it when Em had not seen it herself? And even if she had wanted to turn to writing in those years, would her condition have allowed her the space and concentration to do so?

Or was the writing a manifestation of the condition? It often seemed like it was, the letters growing larger and larger until there was barely a word or two on a page. If we had cared to, we could have mapped her mania against her font size.

There's nothing in Em's diaries or scattered notes about the first time she went out with The Big Hoom. She never hesitated to talk about it, so I wonder if this means something. Or maybe I'm reading too much into it – maybe she did write something and sometime over ten years, or twenty or thirty, that piece of paper was lost. Or it's still in one of her cloth bags and I'll find it if I look hard enough.

The Big Hoom's version was that he had come right out and asked her. She looked frightened, he'd said, and I presume the vulnerability had attracted him.

'The Paranjoti Choir is singing Christmas carols at the American Consulate tomorrow. Would you like to go?'

'I would like to,' said Em. She maintained that she'd meant that she'd have liked to go but not that she'd wanted to go with him. But, she said, it was already too late: 'Before I knew it, he was saying, "We leave the office at seventeen hours tomorrow. Dress up."'

When Em talked about that first date, she seemed to remember her own panic most of all. That single casual instruction – 'Dress up' – had thrown her into a flurry. She had four dresses, all cotton, and one Sunday suit – a coat and skirt with a white lace shirt.

'Surely, you had your Sunday best?' Susan said.

I remember that afternoon clearly. There'd been a scene because Susan, in her first year of college, had announced that a young man had asked her out for a coffee and she'd said yes. Em had shouted at her, asking who the boy was and what business she had saying yes. For a while I feared that

Susan had triggered something and Em would soon be in one of her terrifying manic rages, but Em pulled back from the edge. By the time Susan got dressed, Em was calm. Susan waited for the right time to leave. Em sat in the cane chair by the balcony door and lit a beedi. 'I was your age,' she said, and began to talk of her first date. The tension eased as she told us of her panic, about having nothing appropriate to wear, and Susan asked about her Sunday best.

'Yes, but it looked okay in church. I hated it but it didn't matter once you got to the hall because all the other girls were wearing the same kind of stuff. You fitted in. But I knew I couldn't wear that to the American Consulate.'

'They would laugh?'

'No,' said Em. 'The Americans I met were always polite. They would never laugh. But you knew that if they weren't polite, they would be laughing at you. That's where you're embarrassed. Inside you.'

Finally, Em had consulted Gertrude who had shrugged off the whole sartorial nightmare in a single word. 'Sa-ari,' she had said, drawing out the two syllables to indicate how obvious the whole thing was.

'Such a relief,' said Em. 'Of course, a sari.'

It was a minor matter that she couldn't tie one.

'I would stand in the middle of the room and stretch my arms out and someone would tie it for me.'

There was another problem.

'I could not go to the bathroom. I never did learn how to take a pee in a sari. I mean, the sari and the ghaghra and the pleats and the panties and the seat. It's just too much of a mess.'

Her solution? A total fast.

Gertrude liked the idea. 'It's a good thing to suffer in the beginning,' she said. 'Laugh in the beginning, cry at the end. Cry in the beginning, laugh at the end.'

'He thought I was very bored because I kept sighing. I wasn't sighing. I was trying not to burp. Fasting always makes me want to burp. And there I was, sitting next to the Office Hunk.'

'The Big Hoom?' Susan sounded doubtful.

'What do you lot know? You don't even think *I'm* pretty. But I am, even now, if you would just get that familiarity thing out of your eyes. But I was a looker then, thin waist, big wounded eyes, and the bloom of innocence all over me. And Hizzonner was also quite something in a suit, deep black, and white shirt and glowing sapphire tie to match his eyes.'

'You remember what he wore?'

'He didn't wear that tie. I gave it to him some time later. That day it was a maroon tie. But when I think of him as the hunk, I think of him in a blue tie.'

At the end of the concert, The Big Hoom suggested dinner. Gertrude had assured Imelda that it was her duty to refuse. 'He'll ask. Say no. You must say no to everything on the first date or he'll think you're easy. Say no, no, no. But let him take you for coffee and then let him order dinner.'

'I would have done exactly that,' Em said.

'Didn't you ask Granny?' Susan sounded a bit forlorn.

'Mae? Ah, yes, Mae. She was no use at all,' said Em, a little cryptically, and fell silent. Then she looked at Susan, as if noticing her properly for the first time. Susan was wearing midnight blue.

'Is that you? You look charming,' said Em and took her beedi out of her mouth.

Susan looked startled. Compliments were rare at any time. When Em was high, they were oases in the desert.

'Come and sit by me,' Em said.

'Go, go,' I urged Susan in my head but to give her credit, she didn't even hesitate, though Em had refused to bathe or change for three days and had been smoking incessantly. She smelled unbelievably high.

'Only one word of advice,' said Em. 'Do what your heart tells you. It doesn't matter if you make a mistake. The only things we regret are the things we did not do.'

Susan grinned.

'So you're saying I should sleep with him?'

Em did not miss a beat.

'If you love him. And if you want to.'

'It's a first date.' Susan's insouciance began to crumple slightly around the edges. 'How can I know?'

'Then chances are you don't,' said Em. 'But it's a sneaky thing. It can grow on you slowly. One day you're thinking what does his chest look like under the banny and the next day you can't bear the thought of anyone else wondering about his chest. As if you can ever stop people's minds.'

All of which seemed to be going extraordinarily well. Then Em said, 'But if anything should go wrong . . .'

'Like what?'

'Oh, if he should try and rape you . . .'

'Em!'

'It has been known to happen,' said Em. 'Pretend you're

trying to stroke his swollen cock and then give his balls a twist. Then run.'

Susan got to her feet.

'I'll keep that in mind.'

Em retreated too.

'You do that,' she said and lit another beedi.

'Don't look at me like that,' she said when Susan had gone. 'I have to do my duty as a mother.'

She inflected the word with all the rage and contempt she felt for it. It came out *mud-dh-dha*.

Em did not have the standard attitude towards motherhood. She often used the word with a certain venomousness, as if she were working hard to turn it into an insult. On one occasion, when we were chatting about a terrifyingly possessive mother, she suddenly broke into a chant: 'Mother most horrible, mother most terrible, mother standing at the door, mouth full of dribble.'

Suddenly, now, she began to chant the line again.

It had the ring of a litany this time, but also something else.

'What exactly is that?'

'It's how we would choose the den when we were children. Ugh.'

That was it – the sound of a playground.

'Mother at the door, waiting to eat you up. It's a horrible image but maybe it has an element of truth in it, like those Greek myths.'

'Was Granny a devouring mother?'

'I don't know. I'm here, no?'

'Yes.'

'But I'm mad. That must count against her too. Maybe

she did this to me. Do you think I'm that kind of mother? The kind who'd devour her infants?'

'You could be, but . . .'

'Have you never heard of the phrase "a comforting lie"?'

Living with Em, having survived her into adolescence, we'd earned the right to be her equals. 'Will it comfort you?' I said. 'I'll lie if it will.'

'Oh shut up,' she said, waving at me dismissively. 'You would have to make it comforting.'

'How?'

'How? How? A well-told lie can heal. Otherwise, what's fiction?'

'Okay. You could never be a devouring mother.'

'I don't think a comforting lie can be told after the truth. I'd have to be desperate to accept that. So you can tell the truth.'

'I think you could have been but you lost your chance.'

'Don't be too sure. I could still give it a shot.'

'I don't think you'd have the nerve.'

'Are you challenging me?'

'No, I'm complimenting you.'

'Well, make it a compliment then.'

'Okay. I don't think you could be the kind of person who would go around trying to fuck someone's life up.'

'Is that what you think Mae did?'

'I don't know. I don't think all those terrible women who destroy their children actually look at their babies and say, "Your life is mine. I'm going to maim it." '

'Oh don't,' Em shuddered slightly. 'Marriage is all right. At least the person you're having a go at is an adult. But motherhood . . . You're given something totally dependent,

47

totally in love with you and it doesn't seem to come with a manual. I remember when Lao-Tsu was born . . .'

Lao-Tsu was how she referred to Susan. It came from Sue to Tsu – in some letter she had written to us of an afternoon – to Lao-Tsu.

'. . . the doctor showed me how to carry her, to feed her, and I thought, "I should know this stuff, shouldn't I?" I mean, all those dolls. They were about learning the ropes, no?'

Em lit another beedi. She contemplated the floor.

'She's grown up now. I must confront that. I must see her as men see her. But how can I? I'm hardly the expert on the subject. I only knew three men well – my father, your father and you. And two of you I didn't fuck so that leaves me with your Big Hoom. I'm the world expert on him but who's asking.'

'I am.'

'You are. You are. But you want information. I want to give advice. Experts should be asked for advice. Who would need advice on him? Maybe his mistress. If he ever had one.'

'For a moment there . . .' I began, but stopped.

'Don't be silly,' Em snapped. 'Though I told him once. Mad people don't want sex. They kick the sex drive out of you with those pills. No, even before the pills. There's so much in your head that you can't bear any distractions, you want to pay attention, careful attention, otherwise everything is going to explode. Or something like that. It's like being in a dream where you can do something and every time you try to get it right, you find that the action has shifted to another place and you have to start again. There were times I didn't want sex for months. So I told him, "Get

48

a maid servant. One of those nice buxom girls. She might even teach your son." '

'Me?' I squeaked.

She giggled, a wicked giggle.

'Of course. Fuck the maid, a game for men of middle-class families. Penalty: pissing blood in the morning, that's all. Why should my son be deprived? But he said, "I think he'll find a way to learn about sex without exploiting someone." I hadn't thought of it like that. I suppose it's my upbringing. I thought of it as something men did all the time.'

'To the poske?'

'Yes, to their own adopted sisters, the behenchods. That is what it means, no? I can never remember whether behenchod is sister-fucker or –'

'It is.'

'Keep a mistress, I told him.'

'You didn't mean that.'

'Didn't I though? I don't know. It's very difficult to know what I mean or what I don't mean. Afterwards. At the time, I know.'

'Then how are *we* supposed to know?'

'Osmosis?'

'And how was *he* supposed to know?'

'You're right. How? By the kick of the cow. But he said, "No, if it's okay by you, I'll just stay faithful." What to say to a man like that?'

At the time, I remember wondering why The Big Hoom hadn't taken her up on her offer. I was too young then to figure out the game Em was playing. Today, it seems quite obvious: she was playing out her insecurities. This was allowed by her 'condition'. She could say what other 'normal' women could not.

For one wild moment, I thought I'd challenge her: did she ever repeat that offer? What if he'd been tempted, how could she be sure? But then both of us realized we were very close to the brink and we retreated to familiar territory: the first date, in her version of it.

'What did you eat?' I asked.

'A chicken salad to begin with. And when the edge was taken off, I think I had a ham steak. It was totally gorgeous and what was even better was that he was paying. I wanted to order one more dish but I thought that would be rude so I ate his mashed potatoes as well. And I had a Coke float at the end of it.'

'A Coke float?'

'They would freeze the Coca Cola and put it in a bowl and put a dollop of vanilla ice-cream on top of it.'

'Sounds vile.'

'Don't knock it until you've tried it, buddy.'

'Did he kiss you at your doorstep?'

Em roared, a hoarse rattle in throat and lung. 'I'd have liked to see him try. There was no doorstep in D'Souza Villa, Clare Road, Byculla, Bombay. The door was open, the old ladies of the house were taking the air and saying their prayers and peeking outside. Children were sitting on the steps or playing Mountain-Land-Bridge-Gutter-Sea.'

'So there were no goodnight kisses at all.'

'We were in a taxi. We had to find other places to kiss.'

'What a pity.'

'I don't see why. I don't think the goodnight kiss is such

a hot idea anyway. I mean, why send the poor man off with a hard on? Unless you're a tease.'

It was time to change the topic.

'Didn't The Big Hoom have a car?'

'In those days only the bosses had cars. Or the Parsis. Or the white men. Everyone else used the buses or the trams. But it was a date so we went home in a taxi.'

'Did he at least try? To kiss you?'

'I was frightened to death that he would. I was frightened to death that he wouldn't. But he did the next best thing.'

'What?'

'When we were on Marine Drive, he held my hand.'

'Awww.'

'And well you may say "Aww" because it was perfect. It said, "I want you," but it also said, "I know you're worried about this so I'm willing to wait."'

'That sounds . . .'

'Like I'm thinking up what he thought when he did it? I think we all do that. All women do, at any rate. If I kiss him on the nose, he'll know I love him so I'll kiss him on the nose. We hope he gets it, we fear he doesn't but if he looks even vaguely gratified, we know he's the one.'

'Does it work?'

'What work is it supposed to do?'

'I mean, that "he's the one" stuff?'

'What do I know about men? I've only . . .'

'Yes, yes, you've only had one.'

'Got you there, you foul-mouthed blob of scum. I was going to say I'd only known one well.'

'In the Biblical sense, no doubt.'

'Got me back. Where was I when I so rudely interrupted myself?'

'He took your hand. You thought it was a subtle gesture, coded with many meanings. I wondered about that. You were explaining.'

'That must be a skill you could use.'

'I think it's called being a rapporteur.'

'Does it pay?'

'I suppose. I don't know.'

'Not much use then.'

Not much use. The trail was lost and the story had ended. For a while.

4.

'The prayers of mentals'

If there was one thing I feared as I was growing up . . .

No, that's stupid. I feared hundreds of things: the dark, the death of my father, the possibility that I might rejoice at the death of my mother, sums involving vernier calipers, groups of schoolboys with nothing much to do, death by drowning.

But of all these, I feared most the possibility that I might go mad too. If that happened, my only asset would be taken from me. Growing up, I knew I did not have many advantages. I had no social skills. I had no friends. I had no home – no home that was a refuge. I seemed to have no control over my body; my clumsiness was legendary. All I had was my mind and that was at peril from my genes.

Em's manic state was often ugly but it is how I remember her: as a rough, rude, roistering woman. In this state, she came at us as an equal. But it was the other Em who was my night terror. As if it were a wild animal with flecks of foam at its mouth, I feared her depression.

I found it hard to reconcile the way that word felt to the state my mother was in when she was dragged down into the subterranean depths of her mind. Depression seemed to suggest a state that could be dealt with by ordinary means, by a comedy on the television or an extravagance at a nice shop. It suggested a dip in level ground where you might stumble, but from which you might scramble, a little embarrassed that it should have caught you unawares – a little red-faced from the exertion – but otherwise unharmed.

Em's depressions were not like that.

Imagine you are walking in a pleasant meadow with someone you love, your mother. It's warm, and there's just enough of a breeze to cool you. You can smell earth and cut grass, and something of a herb garden. Lunch is a happy memory in your stomach and dinner awaits you – a three-course meal you have devised – all your comfort foods. The light is golden with a touch of blue, as if the sky were leaking.

Suddenly, your mother steps into a patch of quicksand. The world continues to be idyllic and inviting for you but your mother is being sucked into the centre of the earth. She makes it worse by smiling bravely, by telling you to go on, to leave her there, the man with the broken leg on the Arctic expedition who says, 'Come back for me; it's my best chance,' because the lie allows everyone to believe that they are not abandoning him to die.

Some part of you walks on and some part of you is frozen there, watching the spectacle. You want to stay but you must go. The imperium of the world's timetable will allow you to break step and fall out for a while, but it will abandon you, too, if you linger too long by your mother, now a curled-up foetal ball, moaning in pain, breathing only because her body forces her to.

The only way to deal with such pain is to blot it out. My mother is now in a state where her mind tortures her. It will not even let her sag into apathy. Sometimes I see her body twitching a little in pain. Sometimes I see her forcing herself into a rigid stillness. Nothing will help her answer whatever savage questions her mind is asking.

This is darkness and all that we have as remedy are pills. They don't work. Not when she is this way. My mother lives through the long black night of the mind. She longs for death. She asks us if we can give it to her.

'Kill me,' she says on days when the pain is so bad that she is panting with it, small barely audible sobs. 'Let me die.'

I don't know what to do or how to respond. I want to kill her. I even know how I will do it. First some very strong drugs, of which there is a readily available supply. Then, when she is sleeping, her breath stertorous, a pillow. I run it as a thought experiment, just as I might run the 'What will I do when my father dies' experiment. I don't think I will be able to hold her down if she flails, so I'm hoping that the drugs will make her quiescent.

But I also know that I will not do this. (I wonder if she knows this too and that is the reason why she asks.) I will not do this because I know that she is coming up now. This is the worst of it and it can only be a couple of days more before she begins to surface. These will be days when The Big Hoom will sit by her bed and she will hold his forearm as he reads the paper. From time to time, she will say, 'Mambo?'

And he will put down the paper and look at her.

'Nothing,' she will say.

And he will begin to read again.

For two or three days, we will all live with the knowledge that one of us is gulping for air, swallowing sobs, experiencing pain that will not let up. We will rearrange our lives so that someone is always with her. One morning when I am alone with her, I give her five small orange Depsonils, when her prescription says one.

Does it help? I think not.

The only thing that helps is nicotine, but often on these sludge days of small jerks, aching gasps and no tears, too deep now for tears, she cannot even bring herself to smoke more than a few puffs. She pulls hard and then lets go, gives up, throws away the burning beedi and rushes back to bed and curls up again.

I don't know how to deal with this.

Once, in a desperate – why do these words come when I'm talking about me? I have no despair, have had no despair so immense as this – so: once, in a timid attempt to help, I took her hand in mine and sat with her. My motives were mixed. I wanted to help but I had also written the stage directions for myself: 'Enter son, stage left. He looks at her for a moment and then goes and sits by her side. He takes her hand in his and offers her what consolation he can.'

For a while her hand lay limp in mine and she stopped twitching and she stopped gasping and she looked at me and she rearranged her face into a smile.

But this was her, my sensitive and civilized mother, allowing herself to be part of my script. And so we did not sit like that for long because she was acknowledging the gesture of being comforted by pretending to be comforted. The effort was too great, and finally she took her hand away and said, 'Go baba, go do your work,' and then exhaled her relief.

As I exhaled mine.

I don't know how to describe her depression except to say that it seemed like it was engrossing her. No, even that sounds like she had some choice in the matter. It was another reality from which she had no escape. It took up every inch of her. She had no time for love or hate, fatigue or hunger. She slept ravenously but it was drugged sleep, probably dreamless sleep, sleep that gives back nothing.

She went up. She came down. She went up again. We snatched at her during the intervals. There was no way to say when she would be up or when she would be down. Susan had tried to plot her moods against the cycles of the moon and had come up with no conclusive data even after five years. Then she tried to plot them against Em's menstrual cycles but that had revealed nothing either. The only thing we knew was that September was a bad month; she would be manic through the whole of September, manic in a way that made me wonder how I could ever feel pain for her when she was low.

Between each phase of the cycle, we were vouchsafed a period of normal time. This could last for a few days.

'Or a few weeks,' Susan reminds me.

'When did it ever last a few weeks?'

'The dawn of Lithosun,' she says.

Lithosun. How could I have forgotten? Just when the pharmacopeia seemed fixed, lithium carbonate came into our lives. Li_2CO_3. At first, The Big Hoom seemed sceptical, but since close monitoring was worked into the care, he agreed and the first prescriptions were written.

Lithium was indeed the miracle drug. For two years, Em did not suffer the terrors of twitching depression, nor were her manic states stratospheric. This did not make her an ordinary mother. She still refused to have anything to do with the kitchen. She still thought baths were a necessary evil and tried, like the boys of hundreds of American cartoons, to avoid them. She still laughed immoderately and wondered aloud whether there would be news in the paper about trees because there was a white light shining out of the subabul outside our balcony. But we could all live with this and we settled down happily and humdrummily. We could taste our happiness.

Every month Susan or I would take her for a blood test because lithium carbonate was a poison and could not be allowed to accumulate in her body. Like so many medical tests, this one had to be conducted on an empty stomach. So, early in the morning, armed with a flask of tea and some sandwiches, we would set out for Breach Candy Hospital.

What was it about hospitals that made Em so calm? She was always civil to the doctors and nurses and only once in every while would the mania flash out. In the depressive phase, she was terribly, horribly polite, often begging for forgiveness from total strangers and, more often than not, receiving puzzled benisons.

But during the Lithosun period, she was always ready for a little chat. She would try to draw other patients out, specially the quiet women in the waiting rooms.

'What's wrong with her?' she would ask the husband if the wife could not be teased out of her cocoon of stubborn silence.

'Nerves,' the husband would reply briefly.

'Come home and give her a hug,' my mother would say. 'Take her to the pictures and hold her hand.'

Most of the time, the men took these comments in their stride. Some smiled condescendingly, some looked discomfited but said nothing. Those who suffer from mental illness and those who suffer from the mental illness of someone they love grow accustomed to such invasions of their privacy. Does that make things easier? For everyone? I'm still not sure. I used to wonder: what must it mean for a lower middle-class woman to tell a stranger about her sexual history and her fantasy life? Does she understand the free association that is sometimes used, or why the psychiatric social worker wants to know so much about her childhood? Those who have some experience with homoeopathy may not be shaken or shamed by the bizarreness of the questions, but which Indian woman will talk about masturbation? And what can mental health mean in a nation that wants an injection to put it back on its feet the next morning?

By day, the Breach Candy Hospital catered to the affluent. In the early morning, the place was different. That was the time a wide range of patients turned up, from those who needed their toxins monitored to young men taking a second physical examination in the hope that the results of the first would be invalidated – or at least declared an aberration. Em loved the unexpectedness of the hospital.

'What are you waiting for?' she once asked a morose young man who was thumbing through a thin file.

'I want to go to NDA, aunty.'

'So why aren't you going?' she asked him.

'They are saying I have albumen in my urine.'

'Is that like egg white?'

'I don't know, aunty. But they are not allowing.'

'Have you prayed?' Em asked. This seemed unnecessary since he was well anointed with sandalwood paste and turmeric and there were a few grains of rice still sticking to the red oxide of iron on his forehead.

'Yes aunty. I have promised to write God's name one lakh times if I get into NDA.'

'What is this NDA?'

The young man looked startled. 'Aunty! You don't know? It's National Defence Academy.'

'Oh.' Em was not sure she approved but she rallied. 'I will pray that you get to do what is right for you.'

'What about you, aunty?'

'I had a nervous breakdown and tried . . .'

I began to hiss a little at such promiscuous revelation.

'Don't mind my son. He's shy. I tried to kill myself so I have to take pills and they have to examine my blood.'

'You are mental, aunty?'

I bristled but my mother didn't seem to mind.

'Yes, yes.'

'Oh good. My Buaji says God listens to the prayers of mentals because they are touched by His hand.'

'How nice. You hear that, baba? I was touched by the hand of God. And I have a hotline to Him, according to this young man's someone or the other. I will pray right now.'

'Only . . .'

The young man hesitated. He seemed to be assessing us. Then he took the plunge.

'My Buaji is Muslim.'

'And I am Christian. And you are Hindu. So?'

'Means . . .'

'He's wondering whom you will pray to,' I said to Em. She looked at me. Then at him.

'I will pray to your Buaji's God, then. I'll pray to Allah,' she said.

Did she? I would have prayed to any god, any god at all, if

60

I could have been handed a miracle, a whole mother, a complete family, and with it, the ability to turn and look away.

I lost my faith as an hourglass loses sand. There was no breaking moment but one day I found myself reading the Gospel without a twinge. I had always hated the Gospels because they had unhappy endings, all four of them. They seemed rushed stories. He's born. He grows up. He preaches. He cures. He saves. All this is in the course of a few chapters. And then that Thursday and Friday, the horror of his foreknowledge, the last desperate plea to be permitted to elude this ordeal, the abandonment by friends who cannot keep vigil with him, the humiliation of his nakedness, the pain of the scourgings and the crown of thorns, the mocking crowds, the crying women, the cross, the crucifixion and even the last request – 'I thirst' – denied. I had always felt genuine distress at all this. I could not bear to read it, could not bear to put it down. It was the pain of empathy, the sorrow that this should happen to anyone.

That pain vanished one day. I read the passion through to check myself again. I read another version by another evangelist and was left unmoved. I remember being vaguely relieved and slightly guilty. I did not even realize at that moment that I had lost my faith. What I had left was a syrupy sentimentality and an aesthetic appreciation of the Gregorian chant, the form of the fasting Buddha, and a love of stories. This is the standard equipment of the neo-atheist: eager to allow other people to believe, unwilling to proselytize to his own world which seems bleaker without God but easier to accept.

No one could offer any explanation for the suffering

I watched my mother go through. Nothing I read or heard fitted with the notion of a compassionate God, and God's compassion, one uncomplicated, unequivocal miracle of kindness, was the only thing that could have helped. The sophisticated arguments of all the wise men of faith – their talk about the sins of a past life, the attachment to desire, the lack of perfect submission – only convinced me that there was something capricious about God. How could one demand perfect submission from those who are imperfect? How could one create desire and then expect everyone to pull the plug on it? And if God were capricious, then God was imperfect. If God were imperfect, God was not God.

But being an atheist offers a terrible problem. There is nothing you can do with the feeling that the world has done you wrong or that you, in turn, have hurt someone. I wavered and struggled for a long time before I exiled myself from God's mansion.

I had stopped going to church for a while before that, but when anyone required me to go, whether as escort or mourner or celebrator, I went without demur or comment. The only change I made was in my recitation of the creed which I boiled down to four words: I believe in Jesus Christ.

Because I did. I believed in him and the Buddha and Krishna and Allah because you can believe in anything if you look straight at the message.

Love one another? Good idea.

Detach yourself? Good idea.

Do your duty? Good idea.

Submit to the will of God and go with the flow? Good idea.

In a perfect world, you could even play with permutations and combinations of the above.

Submit to the will of God because he wants you to love everyone and do your duty.

Or, alternatively, detach yourself from everyone as an act of duty to God's will and you will experience perfect and equal love.

It is difficult to see how detachment and love might fit together but the Greeks had a go with *agape*. Only, they didn't use it much, just coined the term and left others to bother about the repercussions of loving someone else with benevolent detachment. It wouldn't work for me. I have to connect to love. I am imperfect, my world is imperfect, I have no time for solutions premised on perfect persons seeing the perfection of solutions that work in a perfect world.

None of my friends would have been surprised by my loss of faith. Most of them were atheists via Marx or Freud and others were agnostic. The few who professed any faith at all hedged it around with disclaimers involving words like meaning, quest and spirituality. No one pushed them to explain. The coyness with which Victorians had approached the sexual was translated into the discomfort with which we approached God. These words were the equivalent of the frilly pantalettes with which the Victorian bourgeoisie covered the legs of their pianos. The mess of faith, the joylessness of disbelief, all these were covered up.

Perhaps that's unfair. All the words about the really important things become chiffon representations of themselves soon enough. Some can be reinvented but others can only be discovered by a personal encounter. Love is a hollow word which seems at home in song lyrics and greeting cards, until you fall in love and discover its disconcerting power. Depression means nothing more than the blues, commercially-packaged angst, a hole in the ground; until you find its black weight settling inside your mother's chest, disrupting her breathing, leaching her days, and yours, of colour and the nights of rest.

But in the summer of lithium carbonate, things were different. Em and The Big Hoom had begun to go out for dinner again. They had started taking walks in Shivaji Park together – short ones in Em's lower phases and longer ones when she was feeling active. They would return with something to eat – fruit sometimes, or a big packet of sev-ghantia – as if we were children. We played along, eating bananas or crunchies as if offered a rare treat.

Then it was over.

One day, Susan came home and Em was at the door. She was snarling slightly, under her breath.

'Come in,' she said to Susan. 'Come in and get behind me.'

'What is it?'

'Nothing,' Em said. 'Come on then, ya bastards. Come and try what you want. You can't take her without getting past me first.'

'Who writes your dialogue?' Susan asked. Oddly, that penetrated the thick red mist.

'Do you want some tea?' she asked.

'Yes,' Susan said and watched as Em stood staring at the pot.

'Come and sit down and have a samosa,' Susan said.

Em grabbed the samosas and threw them into the dustbin.

'No one is to eat a thing that hasn't been cooked in the house,' she said. 'They might poison us.'

'They' were back. And we went back to the psychiatrists hoping for another drug. There was none. The pharmacopoeia was exhausted; we were back to the old faithfuls – Largactil, Espazine, Pacitane for the highs and Depsonil added on when she was depressed. Only this time, we were depressed.

Granny tried to offer me consolation. She tried to tell me the story of the king who looked at his ring in good times and in bad. On his ring there was inscribed, 'This too shall pass away.' Like so many young people offered this purulence of cliché, I said in my heart, 'Fuck off, you stupid old shit with your chutiya clichés and your kings with rings.' In real time, confronted by my grandmother's much-loved, guilt-worn slow dissolve of a face, I said, 'I'll make tea.'

'I'll have a cup too, you silly bastard,' said my mother. 'Not that you were. He took my hymen with his danda, he did. And then three years later, bang on the dot, there you came. Do you know Susan took ten years off the Limb's life? He was white with fear because of my screams. But you? You just popped. They shouted –"The head" – and there you were. A tit man too. You just found the nipple and latched on. Susan, on the other hand, just wouldn't drink. She must have known, woman to woman, she must have known that they had got to me. Don't let them get at the tea. They'll send beautiful girls who will try to bamboozle you.'

'What Imelda . . . ?' Granny tried to stem the tide.

'You don't know anything, Mae. You don't know anything. You don't know how *they* work.'

'Who is . . . ?'

'They target young men. They work on them through the sex instinct. It's very strong in young men. Do you know,

65

Mae, I read somewhere that women peak later but men come into their sexual prime at the age of eighteen. What do you think he would have been like at eighteen?'

'The king with the ring?' I asked. It was enough to distract Em from a subject I hated: her sex life with The Big Hoom. She brayed with laughter, demanded another beedi, and asked me whether I was waiting for an embossed invitation from the Queen before I made the tea.

In the kitchen, I could hear Granny trying to convince Em that no one was after her. I felt my rage rise again. Years of this, no, decades of this, had not taught Granny a simple truth. There was no way into my mother's head. Not at this stage. For most of the year, it was possible to carry on a conversation, even to influence her behaviour with ordinary logic. But when she was twitching with despair or riding the crest of a wave of laughter and fury, you could only make contact by mistake.

'How was your day?' Susan asked her once, when she was depressed.

Em sat up bolt upright in bed and then her shoulders collapsed. Her face crumpled like a little girl's and she began to wring her hands.

'Am I a standing red pen?' she asked.

It would be funny many years later. It would become a family symbol for the cross-connections and misunderstandings that happened when our words went through the prism of Em's illness. They turned into something exotic and bizarre, bearing only a surface resemblance to our meanings. But at that moment, the question came out of the pit. It was coated with the animal intensity you see in the eyes of a dog hit by a car and dying on the road.

'No, you're not,' said Susan firmly. She was taking a huge chance.

'Oh thank God, thank God,' Em sighed and lay down again.

Susan looked around the room for red pens. She checked the house for them. 'I was wondering if there was a standing red pen somewhere. I thought: is this some kind of symbol? I thought: you know, she was a teacher. Red pens? Corrections? Right and wrong? I don't know.'

Sometimes it was possible to catch a glimpse of how Em's mind worked. You saw a note somewhere or you saw the name of a book or a headline. But this was not one of those times. There were no red pens in the house. So she asked Em why she thought she was a standing red pen.

'I don't know,' Em ground out. 'I don't know. I wish I knew but I don't know.'

So trying to tell Em that no one was going to poison her tea was simply not going to work. I wanted to say to Granny, 'You'll only make her think you're one of the people who want to poison her.' I didn't have to say it because by the time I brought the tea back for all of us, Em had independently arrived at the same conclusion.

'Oh so they got to you too, huh?'

Then to me: 'Roger, take over.'

Then she made a dismissive gesture.

'You want me to go?' Granny asked, her tone suggesting that no one could want such a thing.

Em laughed again.

'No, the boy will take you out and shoot you through the head.'

Granny's face collapsed.

'Never mind,' I said to her. 'Just think of the king and his ring.'

Em sprayed us both with tea.

'He got you in the gut, you old hound dog.'

I sympathized with Granny but I also felt a deep vexation. She loved Em and she thought that should be enough. It wasn't. Love is never enough. Madness is enough. It is complete, sufficient unto itself. You can only stand outside it, as a woman might stand outside a prison in which her lover is locked up. From time to time, a well-loved face will peer out and love floods back. A scrap of cloth flutters and it becomes a sign and a code and a message and all that you want it to be. Then it vanishes and you are outside the dark tower again. At times, when I was young, I wanted to be inside the tower so I could understand what it was like. But I knew, even then, that I did not want to be a permanent resident of the tower. I wanted to visit and even visiting meant nothing because you could always leave. You're a tourist; she's a resident.

And as all analogies must, this one breaks down too. You would never be able to visit her tower. You would only be able to visit another tower, a quite similar yet independent one. There were no shared towers, no room for more than one person. I heard this often enough in the shared spaces where Em and I waited for test results, new prescriptions, other doctors.

'Nobody knows what I am going through.'

'What I suffer only I know.'

And so on.

Then one day I was sitting next to two polycot-swathed ladies, both of whom had troubled children.

'What days I have taken out, only I know,' said one.

'But Brian has some good days, no? With Terry, can't say when he gets up whether he'll be this way or that way. Got to be on your toes. One day, Dr Menezes came over for Molly, my small one. She had fever, cough-cold, wouldn't go to the clinic, lying down and crying. So I called Dr Menezes for a home visit . . .'

'Two hundred now?'

'Gone to sleep or what? Three hundred now and without pills. Open mouth. Aaahn. Pull this lid, pull that lid, cough for me, ptack-ptack on the chest and write write write. Finished. Three hundred rupees in the pocket and "Send her to the clinic next time" he got the bupka to tell me. I told him, "Doctor, with all this on my hands I got time? Better to spend this than to listen pitti-pitti-pitti all day." So he's saying, "Must take a heavy toll. How come I never see you in the clinic?" And I said, "Doctor, you'll see me when Terry is well. Because I got no time to be sick when he's like that." '

'Brian is not less, let me tell you. One day, I went out, to novenas only, at Mahim church . . .'

'All the way?'

'Got to go, no?'

'You're lucky you got time. I say in the morning, nine times while I'm cooking. Praying, praying, nine times. "Muttering Matilda", that Terry put name for me. I'm saying, "Storming heaven on your behalf on'y." '

'But I made promise. I got to go. I come back and he's

there, taken off everything and standing in the balcony, singing to the sun. What to say? No one comes forward. When
there is something, death, sickness, marriage, whatever it is,
I still put up my hand. Not much I can do but I'm always
putting up my hand. But no one came forward.'

In all this, I saw no real pain, only a need to demonstrate
one's tolerance and generosity and deep Mother Courage-
ousness. I saw a desperate desire not to affirm each other or
to cling together but to establish a clear hierarchy of suffering. Brian does so-and-so. Well, Terry does such and such.
You were up all night? I haven't slept for a week. I'll concede
now that I was being unfair. I was guilty of hierarchy myself:
I handle it better than them, I suffer with greater grace, I
don't show it. But at the time, I listened to the ladies and it
filled me with anger and contempt.

I had thought once of starting a support group for carers,
for those who lived with the mentally ill, but this kind of
conversation unnerved me. In the days before the Internet, I
put an ad in the papers. I didn't get as many responses as I
had thought I would. One woman would turn up, but only
if the group were Jungian. Another thought that it was a
place where she could leave her brother while she took a
break. A third wanted us to petition the government to set
up more mental hospitals. Yet another said the group should
be anonymous and modelled on the Alcoholics Anonymous. No one could agree on the time and the place and the
date. When we finally did agree, three people came. They
wanted the names and numbers of institutions to which
they could consign their relatives.

'I need a place for my half-brother. I can't look after him

forever. There's no blood tie,' said a lady in a blue sari with a matching bag.

'I think I might go mad and then what will happen to her?' said a retired bank clerk of his wife.

'You should fight this feeling,' said the lady in the sari.

'Fight your genes,' The Big Hoom said to us once, to Susan and me. He did not explain. He did not know how to. But we knew what it meant. It meant that we were to march into the hall and take out our school books and reproduce the slipper-shaped animalcule whose pseudopodia power it through a world without feeling; to learn how to inscribe a hexagon into a circle without tearing the paper; to assimilate the causes and consequences of the battle of Panipat without ever identifying your own enemy because that would mean identifying yourself.

'Fight your genes'. Focus. Be diligent. Concentrate. Do.

The Big Hoom and Susan are discussing historic battles for some reason. I decide to interrupt, feeling left out. Then we hear her.

'I only remember two names of battles. Both have water in them for some reason: Waterloo and Panipat.'

She's saying something of her own accord. She's saying something that's not 'Oh God, Oh God'; something that's not 'Let me die, let me die'. Somewhere a helicopter is landing and the rescue team is beginning to attach straps to her body. She's being airlifted from that Arctic floe; she's being dragged free of the sucking earth. Summer is back.

'The ABC professions'

There's a memory I have from the year I was sixteen. At Christmas Mass, I remember a priest talking about Saint Joseph. The shadowy figure of the father of the incarnate Lord, he called him, and I lost him after that as he maundered on about the virtues of the Holy Family. It was obvious that no one thought much about fathers and fatherhood. Maternity was central.

It wasn't. Not in my world. The Big Hoom was my rock and my refuge. He knew what to do, how to handle stuff. He knew when to let us off and take things over. I tried imagining my life without him and immediately grew cold with fear. I had no idea how one earned money. I knew that one went to work, but what kind of work could I do? When I was asked, I said I wanted to become a doctor but that was ambition by the numbers. Boys of my age, of my social class and academic success, said they wanted to be doctors or engineers. There *were* no other professions in the world, no other professions to which one might aspire. There was only the building of bridges and the repairing of bodies.

But the real fear was not that I wouldn't know how to earn money. It was this: life without The Big Hoom meant life with Em on her own – no, life with Em and no buffer. What if I had to open another door to find that she had sawed at her wrists with one of the knives we had blunted? How would I judge how much blood she had lost and whether she needed a blood transfusion or not? Could that be administered at home? If she died, would I know whom to bribe and how to bribe to make sure it would not turn into a police case? And where would I find the money to bribe, in the first place? What if I put all our savings in a risky business that failed?

At that point I realized what it meant to be a man in India. It meant knowing what one could do and what one could only get done. It meant being able to hold on to two patterns simultaneously. One was methodical, hierarchical, regulated and the outcomes depended on fate, chance, kings and desperate men. The other was intuitive, illicit and guaranteed. The trick was to know when to shift between the patterns, to peel the file off a table and give it to a peon, to speak easily of one's cousin the minister or the archbishop. I did not think I would ever know what these shifts entailed, and that meant, in essence, that I was never going to grow up. Or, and a goose walked over my grave, I would only grow up when The Big Hoom died. Only then would I learn how to deal with the world, this city, this life.

But how did one acquire such knowledge? Did it arrive in the moment itself, the understanding that this was not a man to be suborned, that this was a man who could be subverted? How did other people manage? There must be different ways for every level of society, that much I knew. But what was the way for the son of a mad woman, a 'vedi' in the schoolboy argot of the playground? Anger didn't show the way. Nor hurt.

So how had *he* managed? How had The Big Hoom grown

to the estate of masculinity? Most days I saw him as the perfect man, even in his dense silences that could leave you bleeding for a word in either direction. Then I would correct myself, slowly brutalizing him and so myself and my family. No, he was not a paragon. A paragon would also have been good-looking and would not have thick glasses, passing on to his children the myopia that would have them in spectacles before they were in their teens. Perhaps a paragon might have spotted what was wrong with Em before he married her. A paragon would have been more than a mere crisis manager. And a paragon would have expressed his feelings.

Had Em been the able parent, would things have been different?

This was an exercise that defeated me so completely that I was forced to recognize that The Big Hoom was indeed my paragon. Perhaps I did not want to recognize it only because it made me like every other boy I knew. But they somehow overthrew their fathers or dethroned them or got past them. There was no getting past The Big Hoom.

The Big Hoom's story has the mythic resonance of India in it. I might never have found out, never asked him about it, had it not been for a trip to Goa that we made together. Why weren't Susan and Em there? I don't know. I don't remember. It was not a funeral, it was just something that happened. Perhaps The Big Hoom himself had engineered it.

On the second day, after he had been cried over by sundry old women, most of whom would remain nameless to me, we went for a walk together in the village to which he had never shown much desire to return. Em said it was something to do with the property. He had signed away his rights to prevent a family feud turning into a court case. It hadn't helped and he was now a Goan with no land in Goa.

He was wearing a banian with his office trousers, an odd combination, while I loped beside him, a clumsy fourteen-year-old, unsure of what it meant to be on a holiday with my father, alone. The phrase 'male bonding' was far in the future.

He stopped after we had walked half a furlong, or some distance I imagined to be half a furlong, and looked up at a tank that had been erected on two brick columns with a metal rod, about six feet long, hanging between them.

'When Mr Fernandes built that tank, it seemed like the ultimate modern contraption. Everyone came from miles around to see it being built. Now, it looks like a giant with his dong hanging out of his pants.'

He startled a giggle out of me, because he did not use words like dong. He didn't respond and we walked down a thirsty path, all red mud and stones.

'This was a green and shady walk when I was a boy,' he said. 'They've cut down all the trees.'

The church appeared somewhere to our left.

'That was the biggest building I saw before I went to the Basilica in Old Goa,' he said. 'That's probably why I went to Bombay from Poona.'

'Poona?

'I went to Poona to sit for what you would call a board examination. It was like another planet: a huge world of cars and buses and cycles and noise. On the first day, I felt dizzy at the thought of so many people. All of them looked like they were about to crash into each other but at the last minute they would manage to slip past. It was like watching a hundred games of football going on at once and me in the goal, waiting for a hundred balls, none of which I could see.'

He stopped for a while and then shook his head a little.

'Why did you go to Poona?'

'It was the closest centre for the English examination. I didn't want to study in Portuguese.'

'The language of the overlords.'

'I don't think it had much to do with that,' he said. 'It was just that there seemed to be more jobs available to people who spoke English.'

I fell silent. I felt silly. But then I was fourteen. I could be made to feel silly if someone sneezed.

'There were many boys from Bombay at the school where I was staying. In those days, boys from Bombay would sit for their exams in Poona if they could manage it. I think they felt that the competition would not be as stiff, that they would shine in comparison.'

Among them was Mario, from Dhobi Talao. 'You think this is a city?' he asked scornfully, as the boys sat on the steps of the dormitory of the school. 'Come to Bombay. Now that's a city.'

'I don't know anyone in Bombay,' said Augustine, aged fifteen.

(Was he being disingenuous? Or was he really an innocent from Moira? I didn't ask.)

'You know me,' Mario said grandly. 'Come and see.'

And so it was decided, on the spur of an invitation and a moment, on the challenge of a city vaster and grander than he could imagine, that Augustine would go to Bombay.

'I had money to go home. I used it on a ticket to Bombay. I don't know what I was thinking. Or whether I was thinking about money at all. I had never had any before that, no pocket money, no spending money. Everything I had was second-hand or third-hand or bought for me. So perhaps I thought one could get on without money.'

Mario's mother came to receive him. The Big Hoom was not big on details but I imagined her in the standard garb of the Goan Roman Catholic lower-middle-class housewife. She would have been in a white-ish rayon shirt – not quite white because white is difficult to keep clean, who has the time? – embellished with fake lace. From under the collar, two pink satin ribbons falling limply on her chest. A black skirt riding under her paunch. And on her feet, low slippers that showed her cracked heels and the bunions on her toes. There would have been a faint smell around her, a smell of worry – Mario's exams, husband's alcoholism, Maria's marriage, her own over-strained budget, the leaking bathroom, the troublesome boss who did not understand why she had to take an hour off to fetch her son from the station; the worry that had carved a single deep line between her brows. I realized later that I was dressing her with the contempt of my class and the notions of my time. Rayon would not have been as popular at the time. And that entire outfit was more 1980s than 1950s.

'She took one look at me,' The Big Hoom said, 'and said, "Who is this?" Mario said, "He's Augustine. He's from Goa." "Okay, nice to meet you," she said and took her son and left.'

'Didn't Mario tell her that he had invited you?'

'He turned around as if to say something, I think. Maybe he even said "Sorry aahn?" or something like that. I don't think he ever told his mother that he had invited me to Bombay to stay with them.'

'What did you do?'

Suddenly on that warm Goa afternoon, I felt the cold horror of that moment reach me across the years. The Big Hoom had been about as old as I was. I would not have known what to do. I would probably have burst into tears or gone running after Mario and his mother.

'I stood there for a while. I didn't know what to do. I had very little money left. And then a car stopped in front of the station and a lady got out and said, "Take out those bags." I thought she wanted some help so I got the bags out but when I had carried them into the station, she gave me two pice.'

'Two pice?'

'A grand sum,' said The Big Hoom. 'My first earnings ever. I spent them immediately on tea and an omelette at the railway canteen.'

'So you became a coolie?'

'Who knows what would have happened if I had become a coolie?' The Big Hoom asked reflectively and I promised myself that I would stop my silliness by simply not saying anything more. 'It's like that Maugham story of the illiterate sacristan who gets the sack and becomes a millionaire because he goes into business for himself. A journalist comes to interview him and asks him something like, "You achieved all this and you were illiterate. What would have happened if you were literate?" And the millionaire replies, "I would have been a sacristan."'

Railway coolies were a closed shop.

'You couldn't just pick up a bag and earn a couple of pice.

You had to belong to the fraternity. And to belong to the fraternity, you had to speak Marathi and know someone who already belonged. I could only speak Konkani and Portuguese and English and I knew no coolies. So I was warned and kicked out of the station and went back to get my luggage.'

'Oh God.'

Of course. He would have had to put down his own bags to carry the woman's bags . . .

'The bags were gone. But someone said that they had been handed over to the stationmaster as lost luggage.'

Finally, a stroke of luck. The stationmaster was Goan.

'He made me wait outside his office. He said he would put me on the bus the next day. He took me to the Moira *coor* and bought me dinner. They found a bed for me. In the evening, the men and boys came back. I didn't know any of them but they took me to Cross Maidan and we played football. They bought me dinner too. The cleaners gave me some breakfast and in return, I had to help wash the floor. That was okay. I didn't mind work. At around five, an old man came into the dorm and said, "Where's Pedru?" No one knew where Pedru was. One of the cleaners said, "Patraõ, you know what Pedru's problem is." "Fallen down drunk again?" said the old man, ignoring the fact that he was reeking of alcohol himself. "Such a pity." Then he saw me and said, "You, what's your name?" I told him. "Got a job?" I told him I didn't have one. He switched to Portuguese. "Do you speak Portuguese?" he asked. "I speak it fairly well," I said. "Do you speak English?" he asked. "I speak it well," I said. He switched to Konkani. I could speak that too. Then he switched to Hindi and Marathi and Gujarati but I just kept shrugging. I didn't even know a few words in any of those languages. I thought: "Gone, now I won't get the job." But finally, he shrugged and said, "You'll pick them up, I suppose. Come on, then."

'So I went with Dr da Gama Rosa to his clinic. It was the first time I had ever sat in a car. And when I told him that he laughed and said it was the first of many firsts.'

'What did he want you to do?'

'Oh, didn't I tell you? He was a doctor and he needed a compounder.'

'You were a compounder?' I asked.

'Why not?'

I knew what a compounder was. He was the guy who shelled out the pills, wrapping up your morning, afternoon and evening doses separately, pouring a bit of red syrup into a bottle and adding a bit of pink syrup that tasted of mint. Then the bottle itself would have a label stuck on it and the dose marked on the obverse with a strip of paper. The compounders I knew were all ghostly presences. George, the one who reigned in our family doctor's clinic, was a man whose face I would always remember foreshortened, framed in the circular aperture through which he passed pudias of pills and bottles of syrup. Through the years that we knew him, he said very little. 'Three times a day after meals,' he might say. 'Come back in three days.' Or, 'The white ones are to be stopped if the fever goes.'

Another element of my father's ability to handle the universe fell into place. He had an almost benevolent contempt for Dr Saha, the family physician. When we were ill, we went to The Big Hoom and he told us what was wrong. Most often he would say, 'Go and lie down and only get up to go to the toilet.' He believed in rest, lots of fresh fruits and vegetables and boiled water as a cure for almost everything. If he thought we needed pharmaceutical help, he'd take us down to Dr Saha and try very hard not to dictate the prescription.

Em, on the other hand, needed reassurance that we were not about to die.

'When Susan was a baby,' she told me once, 'she had diarrhoea. She seemed to be doing nothing but shitting. And green shit too. So I covered the floor with a plastic sheet and I spread out all her soiled nappies for Dr Saha to look at.'

'What did he say?' I asked, as the image began to blossom in my head and the sheet grew and more and more diapers began to festoon the room and the smell began to grow, putrid and pungent.

'He gave me that classic look,' she said. It was a classic Em remark. Its origin lay in some advertisement, perhaps for men's clothing.

This was one of my ways of dividing up the world. My mother: incapable. My father: capable. My mother's mind belonged to the humanities. My father was the engineer. I was so used to talking about my father as an engineer, I was a little startled to think of him as a compounder. I had no idea I took any pride in his calling. I liked to think I would have been proud of him as a street sweeper but that, I knew, somewhat uncomfortably, was so hypothetical as to be impossible to imagine. And now the thought of him as a compounder had me thinking.

'What happened to Pedru?'

'He came back once, very drunk. The doctor sent him away. "Both of us can't be drunk, Pedru," he said.'

'The doctor was an alcoholic?' I asked.

'Yes,' said The Big Hoom. 'He was drunk almost all the time. There was nothing much to do since hardly anyone would come to him and so he drank more. There were a few patients who still believed in him, but most of the others wanted a man who didn't smell so strongly of alcohol at ten in the morning. But that was a pity because he was a great doctor. He listened. He took notes. He made out careful case histories. He kept records. He made house calls. He kept secrets. He never prescribed because a medical representative had promised him an incentive or had given him a wall clock. He had some raisins in his desk drawer for children. He washed his hands after every patient. And he would not laugh at Ayurveda or Unani or homoeopathy. "Sometimes, they get in the way less than we do," he would say.'

This made me slightly uncomfortable. I had discovered The Big Hoom's hero. I did not want my hero to have a hero.

'He made me read to him from the papers every day and from *Reader's Digest*. "They put in a load of rubbish," he would say, "but you can learn something and you can learn the language well." He believed in English. "It is the new Latin," he would say. "Because of America. All the new inventions come out of America and so everyone has to learn English."'

'One thing . . .' I started.

'One thing,' he said. 'If you want to get people to talk to you, you should never interrupt.'

'Never? Even if I think something is wrong or missing?'

'Especially if you think something is wrong or missing.'

'Why?'

'Stops them. Gives them time to think. Interrupts the flow. If you want to get more, you shut up and wait.'

And so did I get my first lesson for life as an adult from my father. I remained silent until he raised his eyebrows in a mute question.

'Why didn't you go home? Dr da Gama Rose . . .'

'Rosa.'

'Whatever.'

'No, his name was Dr da Gama Rosa. Names are import-ant. Isn't yours important to you?'

My second lesson.

'He'd have given you the money to go home. Or you could have earned it with your first salary.'

'I suppose,' my father said. 'I could have. But I didn't. Why didn't I? I don't think anyone has ever asked me that before. No, I don't think I've asked myself that question before. That's a good question, then. I didn't go home. I stayed.'

He thought about it for a while. I felt important, and I felt silly that I was feeling important.

'I suppose I was ashamed. I had been stupid. I had taken a boy's invitation and come to the city. I had lost all my money. And maybe it was because everyone who came back from the city, came back rich. They went to Bombay or Aden or Nairobi and they came back with stories of things they had seen or what they had done. I would have had to say that I went to the city and became a coolie and a compounder and had come home.'

He fell silent again. I was minding my manners and my lessons in life, so I was quiet and was rewarded.

'Or maybe it was simpler. Maybe it was ambition. Maybe

83

it was the city. I don't think you'll ever understand how challenging the city can be for a boy from a village. You don't know anything about it. You don't know if you buy your ticket before or after you get onto the train. You don't know if you can go into a mosque or not. You don't know if the man holding out booklets is offering them free or is selling them. You don't know why a stranger is smiling at you from the next park bench.'

'Wouldn't that make you want to run away from it all?'

'That's where pride comes in, and stubbornness. The city is a challenge but it's a challenge that doesn't care either way. If you go home, it won't jeer, it just won't notice. You can stay and work hard and make something of yourself and it still won't notice. But you will know. I would have known that I had failed. So I stayed.'

'You could have written,' I said. It was family legend that Masses had been held in the village church for my father's soul. The family had assumed he was dead.

'They thought I had died in Poona or on the way back.'

'Why not on the way there?'

'Because my examination results came in the post. I did well too.'

That must have fitted in nicely with the tragedy, I thought.

'When did you return?'

'With my engineering degree.'

As the doctor's practice declined, he began to invest more and more of his life into his compounder's future.

'We work in the ABC professions,' Dr da Gama Rosa said. 'Ayahs. Butlers. Cooks.'

'Doctors too,' said his compounder.

'Drunks, more likely,' said the Doctor. 'If you want to be someone else, you have to work ten times as hard because they see us as the boys in the band. But what's worse is that that's how we see ourselves. Do a little work, sing a song, drink yourself to death, go out with a funeral band and four children following the coffin.'

Once his assistant had begun to master the English newspapers, the doctor made him read a series of English classics borrowed from a public library that stood at the corner of Dhobi Talao. At first, Dr da Gama Rosa picked the books but eventually he started sending The Big Hoom.

'One day, I happened to look over a young man's shoulder and saw a cutaway drawing of a motor. I did not know what it was at the time but it looked fascinating. So I asked him what the book was and he flipped it over so I could see the cover. It was Coates' Manual for Engineers. I wanted to ask him more but he said he was studying for an exam, so please. I looked at the shelves and found another Coates. It was marked 'for reference only' but Dr da Gama Rosa had told me how to get around that. Most of the time the labels were old so all you had to do was peel it off and get the book issued anyway.'

'What did the doctor say when you started reading Coates?'

'I think he was disappointed. I think he wanted me to become a doctor. When I was in the clinic, he would test me all the time. He would make me read temperatures and take blood pressure and ask me what I would prescribe.'

Which explained the almost impersonal kindness with which The Big Hoom treated us when we were ill.

'And so you got into the Victoria Regina Technical Institute?'

'On the second attempt,' said The Big Hoom. 'And three years later, with an engineering degree, I went home.'

The prodigal was not welcomed, even if he had made good.

'Your grandmother was a big woman for her time. She was nearly five foot ten and she could carry a head-load of firewood five kilometres to the Mapusa market, talking all the while.'

The news spread even before he got off the bus.

'By the time I reached home, mother was waiting for me with a stick,' he smiled. 'Later, I was told she had burst into tears at the news, then dried her eyes, killed three chickens, changed her sari and picked up the stick.'

'Did she beat you?'

'No. Six years had passed. She remembered a boy of fifteen who would take his father's shirts without permission. She hit me once or twice but there was no conviction in her. And I remember when she hit me, the village, standing behind, said "Ohhhhh" and then when she hit me the second time, they all said "Aaahhhhh". She got angry and roared at them. "Kaam na?" Don't you have any work to do? And then she took me in to see my father.'

'He didn't come out to see you?'

'He was paralysed from the waist down. We don't know how it happened. He was working as a cook in Hyderabad. My mother said he was in the Nizam's palace, but then everyone in Goa said that they were cooking for royalty if they were cooks. Most of the time, they were cooking for middle-class Parsis in Bombay.'

'Were they happy to see you?'

'I suppose. But I think they were happier when I showed them my degree. Neither could read so my mother brought in a lady from the next house to read it out to her so she could be sure that I wasn't fooling them. Then I showed them the letter from Ampersand Smith Limited, the company I had joined as a trainee engineer.'

'What happened to Dr da Gama Rosa?'

'When I got the job, he said, "Now don't show your face here again." I said that I would come and see him on Saturdays. He said, "We'll see." Of course, that made me all the more determined to go and see him. But when I went on the first Saturday, the clinic was closed. So I went on Monday, sneaking out at lunch. He was pleased to see me and told me to keep two shirts and a pair of trousers at the office at all times.'

'Why?'

'I think he meant that a man had to look fresh at all times. And if the rain got you, you could change.'

It seemed like odd advice but perhaps a drink-sodden doctor felt that any other advice coming from him might seem odd.

We seemed to have reached the church. It was time to turn back. But The Big Hoom kept on walking, lost in thought.

'Did you visit him every week?'

He stopped and looked at me.

'If anyone ever does you a favour, you cannot forget it. You must always credit them, especially in public, especially to those they love and those who love them. You must pay your debts, even those that you can never fully repay. Anything less makes you less.'

But he did not say anything more. He was in the process of taking out a cigarette, a rare pleasure that he allowed himself infrequently, although he always carried a packet around. It was understood that no one was allowed to speak to him when he was smoking, no one except Em.

Anything less makes you less. Was that how it was for him as a husband? She had loved him, and he would never forget it; he would be with her and love her in return, always, even if it wasn't enough.

It is only now that I think of this – of him. Em filled our lives, there was no space in our minds for The Big Hoom. He was our constant, he was perfect, he just was. We were never really curious about his past, or even his present outside our flat.

When did he first sense that his buttercup wasn't whole? I don't know. How did he deal with it when he first discovered that she needed to open up her veins, throw herself in front of a bus? I don't know. How did he deal with it when she turned over in bed and asked him whether showing the Marines her Maidenform underwear would save her children? I don't know.

Perhaps the truth is not that Em extinguished all curiosity about The Big Hoom, but that I, at least, couldn't ask because I was afraid. I thought he might no longer be able to do what he did if he realized he was doing it.

How did he deal with it all? Now, I can only guess: One day I told him about the boys of the neighbourhood, about their mocking.

He said, 'That's because they don't understand.'

'They should understand,' I said. I didn't want to cry, but I was crying.

'If your mother had diabetes, what would they say?'

'I don't know.'

'This is like diabetes. She's not well. That's all.'

Was that what he told himself? That she was not well? That she might get better? I don't know.

6.

'I am no I'

Em, Susan and I were talking about the buying of books. Susan and I assumed that Imelda wanted to buy books on those endless bookshop evenings with Augustine.

'No,' she said. 'I didn't.'

'You just told yourself that because you didn't have the money,' Susan said.

'Did I? Much you know. I didn't want to buy books. And I don't, not now. I don't know if I ever did. I love books. I love reading. The pills took that away from me. They made it difficult.'

'To concentrate?'

'Yes. But that's only sometimes. Most often, they made it difficult to sympathize. You have to care a little and I couldn't because caring would mean letting go.'

'Letting what go?'

She looked at Susan, then at me, with none of her usual defiance. Instead, there was something like bewilderment in her eyes. 'I wish I knew. Sometimes I would see myself as a book with bad binding. You know, like one more reader, one more face-down on the bed and I was going to spill everything, lose control.'

She shrugged.

'I know. What control do mad people have? I don't know myself. I only know there is some control. Some things you can choose not to say. Some things you can choose not to do. It's such a mess, that's why it's madness. Because even when you say things which are not in your control, you're saying them because not saying them will mean having to say other things. So you say, "I'll let this one out of its cage and that should make the other cage stronger."'

She looked at us again.

'Never mind, I'm happy you don't understand. Maybe it does skip a generation.'

I shivered but put the thought away.

'But I liked bookshops,' she said.

And somehow the boy from Moira figured that one out. His own parents had been as close to illiterate as made no difference. His father, as a cook in a palace somewhere out in the Deccan Plateau, could read Urdu. His mother could sign her name on the letters she dictated to him. The only books he had ever possessed as a child were the battered hand-me-down textbooks of the English-medium school to which he had been sent.

Perhaps that was why he loved books so passionately.

'There's a book sale on,' Augustine would announce in passing to Imelda, as he whirled by her desk in ASL.

I remember Em saying, 'He always looked like he was in a hurry. Not that he ran, but he seemed to move very fast, like Mercury. So when he slowed down and took his time to chat to you, the effect was devastating.'

I tried to imagine The Big Hoom like that. I couldn't. Had she slowed him down? Had we?

There weren't many bookshops in the days when Imelda and Augustine were young. And in the bookshops, there weren't many buyers. Just lovers, long-distance lovers.

'I didn't go to bookshops to buy. That's a little bourgeois. I went because they were civilized places. It made me happy there were people who sat down and wrote and wrote and wrote and there were other people who devoted their lives to making those words into books. It was lovely. Like standing in the middle of civilization.'

I rolled my eyes. Susan glared at me. Em didn't seem to care. She was picking idly at the edge of her dress and a part of me wondered if this was only her reverie or an early warning sign of a bout of depression.

'I went to bookshops to smell that lovely aroma of a new book. I would pick up a copy and run the pages across the ball of my thumb and let the fresh-baked smell flow up my nose. Then I would lick my thumb. It didn't taste of anything, but it was like finding a chocolate wrapper inside a book and remembering the taste of the chocolate.'

'You put chocolate wrappers into books?'

'Indeed we did. Not just any old chocolate. Special chocolate. Chocolate from abroad. Chocolate your best friend gave you.'

'As a bookmark?'

'No, not as a bookmark. As remembrance. That should you never get chocolate again, you would know you had once eaten this bar.'

It seemed odd.

She read my mind. ('Mad people are telepathic, clairvoyant and everything that should frighten you. Be afraid of me,' she had once joked.)

'Yes, I was a little odd even back then – I must have been, no? In fact, I think we were both odd. We did not go to buy. We went to bookstores because they were high-ceilinged rooms with slow-turning fans. We went for the evening light and the shelves full of lovely things. We didn't have quite as many things back then. Things like these,' she said, pointing to the bowl of glass toffees a cousin had brought us from Prague. 'I can't imagine why anyone would make glass toffees when real toffees in a bowl make people so much happier. What do glass toffees mean?'

'I think they're supposed to be for ironic amusement,' I said.

'Gosh. No, I don't think there was a shop full of ironic amusements.'

She picked up a glass toffee and twirled it between her fingers.

'When you two are not here, I'm going to raise an eyebrow at them and look ironically amused.'

We giggled together. Em set down the toffee.

On days like this – no, at moments like this – it was quite possible to forget all the tags – mad, manic depressive, bipolar – and frolic with her through van Goghian fields of free association.

'There's something brave about a piece of glass that is fated to live its life as a toffee when it could have been a bulb or a thermometer,' she said. 'But I can't imagine anyone window-shopping these days.'

'They do. People say they do it all the time,' Susan assured her.

'I wonder. How can anyone go window-shopping when people actually buy glass toffees? How does one say "That's what I'm going to buy when my boat comes home" when you're already buying whatever you want?'

'I think your budget would constrain you still.'

'It would, I suppose. But window-shopping was tourism once upon a time. You never thought you would take any of that stuff home. You didn't think it would belong to you. Like the Taj Mahal. You went to look at it and then you got a good shot of it running in your veins. You now had some beauty under your eyelids.'

'It was enough?'

'It was enough. You could live with the street on which you lived. I remember I cried when I saw my first vacuum cleaner.'

'Why?'

'I was so glad someone had thought to make something like that. I felt it was a kindness to women everywhere. But I certainly didn't think we could afford one. I don't even think I asked.'

'So you and The Big Hoom just stood in bookshops and read?' I asked to bring her back to where we'd started.

'No. I don't think that was allowed, or even encouraged. Not at Lalvani's or at Thacker's. You could read the back of the book and maybe sniff a few pages, but I remember Mr Lalvani once bearing down on a customer, hissing, "Do you want to damage the spine?" I thought *he* was going to damage that man's spine instead.'

Augustine and Imelda did not start dating at any real point in time. It simply became clear that they were dating. As if by an unspoken agreement, without anyone admitting it, they began to go around.

'Going around? Is that what you call it these days? It makes me dizzy.'

'What did you call it?'

'Dating, I suppose.'

'That's better or what?'

'No, it's stupid. Half dry fruit and half almanac. But I think if The Big Hoom had asked me out on a date, I would have refused.'

'Why?'

'I don't know. I was prudish, I think. We all were. We thought no one would marry us if we weren't virgins. I remember listening to stories about women putting lemon juice there or cutting themselves to bleed and I remember thinking, "What a lot of fuss. So much easier not to do anything at all so you don't have to fake it."'

'But a date was hardly going to end in . . .'

'Yes, yes, I know that now,' she said a little testily. 'But then? In the American magazines, it seemed like there was a strict calendar. You didn't kiss on the first date or you would be seen as cheap and he wouldn't respect you. If you went on a second date and didn't let him kiss you, you were a tease. I thought: "What happens if you meet a man you like to talk to but don't want to kiss?" But you couldn't be like that. You had to let him kiss you and then you could do some necking after that but no petting . . .'

'What's the difference?'

'I think, but don't quote me, necking was above the shoulders and petting was below it.'

'But when did you know?' Susan wanted to know. 'When did you know that he was the one?'

'I don't know. Is there a moment? Like that?' Em asked, snapping her fingers. 'Maybe there is. Let me see. How about a cuppa while I rack my brains?'

Susan obliged, but when she was back, the conversation had wandered somewhere else – to the story of the priest who had fathered six boys and baptized them all because they were his nephews.

It was many years later that I discovered how Imelda knew that Augustine was the one. I discovered it from an old letter she had written a friend, a letter she had forgotten to post but remembered to preserve.

> . . . he breezed into the office with chocolate for one and all. He had a whole bunch of them he had swiped from some swanky do to which he had been invited. Though Gertie says no one says 'do' any more because it's common. It's common? Well, so be it. If I had had the good sense to write in pencil, I might have made myself uncommon and corrected that to 'party', but 'party' sounds like something with cake and cold drink. And 'function' sounds like a bunch of local yokels making speeches. Well, whatever. I shall say 'do' if I want. Begone, Gertie.
>
> Where was I? Ahn? (Anh? Aahn? Nothing looks right.) The chocolate mints. I'm writing this letter in fits and spurts because Mae is fluttering around looking like she's about to rearrange the furniture, while I'm trying my best to be the immovable object against which the irresistible force must expend itself. Or must it? I don't know. Will ask Him Who Knows All About Engineering. And promptly forget.
>
> Oh stop it! I'm doing it again.

And now Mae's saying it is time for my bath, which is a sure way of making me plant myself . . .

She won. She always does. She said I was beginning to smell. So I went and had a bath that was a lick and a promise, but when I came back All Was Lost and I had no Alternative But to Flee and am writing to you now in the Irani café at the end of the lane with the beady eye of Mr Ghobadi on me. He knows me too well to uproot me when my tea is done and the last crumb of mawa cake wiped from my plate, but he resents the occupation of his space without the earning of some pounds and pence and pice.

As I was saying.

The mints went down nicely with all the girls. (I did mention that the chocolates had mints in them, non?) But Audrey was not among those accounted for. She had stepped out to buy some feminine sanitary products. I wish there was a nice word for them things. Pads? I suppose. Okay, she went out to buy some pads and did not get her share of the goodies. Of course, Gertie had to rub it in. Gertie has had it in for her ever since Audrey announced the nuptials. She can't bear it. When Audrey asks us whether we prefer mauve gauze or pink tulle for the bridesmaids, her joy turns to ashes in her mouth.

So Gertie rubs it in: 'None for you, poor dear?' And then he fetches up at my desk and says, 'We have a problem.'

I handed over my chocolate because I knew what the problem was. And anyway, couldn't tell him, but those chocolates with mint in them taste like toothpaste. He grinned and winked and bounced off to make Aud feel less like the odd one out. (I worked out that pun. I know one is supposed to say, 'Forgive the pun,' but I worked it out so why should I ask forgiveness? The English language is very complicated, hein?) And when I was on my way home that evening – he was off on another client meeting – I realized that I had plighted my troth over a chocolate mint. I am no I. I am now part of a we. Wee wee wee, I wanted to weep and run all the way home and bury my head in my mother's lap. Not that . . .

The fragment ended there.

Most of what I know about their love came from Em in her garrulous phases, and the occasional letter or scrawl in one of her diaries that she showed me. Little of it came from The Big Hoom. Not because he was a man of few words – he was a salesman and could talk the milk into butter, as they said in Moira – but he does not seem to have wasted too many on his Beloved. His letters to her are classic 'male' letters. This one was written before they were married; he was away on a buying trip to France.

Beloved,

Arrived in Paris to weather that to my subtropical body seemed intolerably cold. Yet the young lady waiting at the airport to receive her boyfriend was wearing a mini skirt. I took pains not to notice this, but it did rather obtrude upon the consciousness.

I will be meeting with several of the suppliers. The problem, of course, is that we would like to deal with the Europeans but the government of India would like us to deal with the East Europeans. It's a matter of bloc politics. Now, I was going to suggest to the French that they should set up a company, a small independent company with a branch in Prague. We could then deal with Prague and they could invoice us in francs through the holding company. You will point out that the currency is the rub, right? But it seems that the Communist bloc is quite pragmatic about these things; they would like to be paid in dollars so I suppose francs won't upset the government too much.

There is the likelihood also that they might turn this down as too much work. But I think if we promise them an estimated 600 machines in the next three years, that's almost a three per cent increase in their sales. That is why I want to deal with Corbeaux and not Franco. Franco would not get excited at the thought of 600 machines; they'd probably shrug and ask me to do business in the way business should be done.

I miss you very much but I need hardly say that. You would like Paris, I think. There's a casual beauty about it, rather like yours.

All my love,
Augustine

His letters offered little. And Susan and I rarely asked him any questions about their meeting or their romance. By the time we were prying teenagers, The Big Hoom had become one of those solid-as-a-rock men of the world who rarely give the impression that they have a past or a private life.

Their courtship lasted nearly twelve years. Family legend says that they might have gone on for another twelve, perhaps forever. Imelda had moved on from ASL, found a job at the American Consulate that paid much better. Augustine met her outside her office every evening and they walked to their favourite bookshops, and occasionally went to the movies. They were happy enough doing this. But Em had a godmother and aunt, combined in one person, who wielded enormous moral power in the family, and when Em's thirtieth birthday was coming up, her Tia Madrinha Louisa decided to take a hand in the matter of Augustine and Imelda and the bookshops.

One afternoon, two senior women, dressed in silk and magnificent Sunday hats, presented themselves at the offices of Ampersand Smith Limited. They asked to speak to A. G. Mendes and were ushered into his cabin.

'You must forgive us for intruding upon you like this,' said one of them in perfect Portuguese. 'But we are only motivated by the love of the young ones of our family.'

Augustine goggled a bit.

'I am sure you are,' he replied in Portuguese for he had studied the language in school. 'But you will forgive my incomprehension when you realize that I do not know who you are.'

'We are not in the habit of introducing ourselves,' said the older lady. 'I suggest you ask Mr Andrade who works here with you to introduce us.'

Under normal circumstances, Augustine would have simply thrown back his head and roared for Andy. But something told him this might startle the old ladies into dropping their large purses, shiny patent leather objects with wicked golden clasps. He called a peon and asked if Mr Andrade might not be free to drop by.

Andrade came in and sized up the situation in a moment. He put on a formal air and proceeded to make introductions as if the two women had been strolling in the prasa and had come upon Augustine quite by chance. He gestured to Augustine that he should rise to his feet and with the same, almost imperceptible, gesture indicated that it was not necessary for the ladies to rise.

'Dona Bertha, Dona Louisa, may I present my good friend, Augustine Mendes? This young man has a bright future at the sales department here, ladies. And these ladies, Agostinho, are my mother's close friends. She has known them for many years. Perhaps you have some acquaintance with the daughter of one who is also the niece of the other and who worked with us for some years.'

That was when things fell into place for Augustine. Andrade asked to be excused and left.

And so the young engineer was left in his cabin with the battleaxes.

He didn't do too badly. He offered them tea and biscuits. They were very impressed that the biscuits were British. Word had got around. Perhaps Andy had told the staff that it was an important meeting for AGM, a decisive one, and the staff had rallied.

'The Big Hoom told me later that they were very formal and polite,' Em said.

The exchange, from what I have gathered, went something like this:

'Our circumstances are not what they once were,' says the elder woman. 'Bertha was driven from her home in Burma by Herr Hitler. Very little was left.'

'Our chemist shops,' Bertha adds. 'And the this-thing.'

'Teak plantation,' says Louisa. 'She means the teak plantation.'

'That's what I this-thing,' says Bertha. Louisa ignores her.

'I see,' says Augustine, although he doesn't. He hasn't yet learnt his future mother-in-law's conversational style.

'But much wants thissing-thissing,' Bertha says.

'Much wants more,' says Louisa. 'And enough is a feast.'

It becomes clear to Augustine that he is confronted by a double act. (They had always been close, but over time, Bertha and Louisa had got to the point where they could finish each other's sentences.)

Louisa: Where are you from?

Augustine: Moira.

Louisa: That is a good village.

Bertha: Thissing.

Augustine: Pardon me?

Louisa: Christian.

Augustine: Yes, I suppose it is.

Louisa: Are you related to F.X. Mendes of Astora?

Augustine: No, I don't think so.

Bertha: He was our thissing.

Louisa: Father.

Augustine: The editor F.X. Mendes?

Bertha: Yes.

Augustine: I have heard of him.

Augustine is not being facetious. He really has. F.X. Mendes had conducted, through the civilized medium of his newspaper, a case against the toilet of a wealthy brahmin. The facts: the brahmin's home faced a plot, long unused, upon which he had had his eye. One day, he discovered that it had been bought by a man of unquestionably lower caste. He also discovered that the low-caste man was intent on building on his land and was going to build a house, by virtue of funds supplied to him by his brothers who were settled in East Africa and doing 'quite well for themselves', a term by which opprobrium and praise – in equal measure – may be heaped upon those who try to get beyond their station. And to build a house right in front of that of the only rich man in the village – and a brahmin – was an act of hubris that demanded a suitable response. At that time, no one thought much of having an outhouse, a pig toilet at which an eager porcine nose might suddenly meet one's rear end as one squatted. The rich man had a bright idea. He would build an indoor toilet. He would build it so that it came very close to the living room of his new neighbour. He would then fart in the upstart's face each morning.

It was this terrible plan that F.X. Mendes worked to foil. It is entirely likely that he ran other campaigns. It is entirely likely that he opposed Portuguese rule or supported it fervently. No one knows. No one remembers. They only remember that F.X. Mendes fought the toilet case and won it. Depending on who is telling it, there is either admiration at the old man's stubborn insistence on the rights of the poor or incredulity that newspaper columns should concern themselves with such petty matters.

Bertha and Louisa must have both peered into his face to see on which side of the divide Augustine fell. To have a famous father can be a terrible burden.

Augustine: My brothers often said he wrote beautiful Portuguese.

Bertha: He was quite this-thing but now this-thing.

Augustine: He made his mark.

Louisa: Do you speak Konkani?

Augustine (switching to Konkani): I speak Konkani.

He knows there is a slippery patch coming along. (In those days, and among the kind of women who were sitting in front of him, there were those who maintained that Konkani was the language of the tiller of the soil and the bearer of the load. They maintained as well that Portuguese was the language through which Goans could dream of some success in Lisbon where everyone always told them how beautifully they spoke the language. And then there were those who believed that Portuguese was a foreign import that belonged only to a certain community and that Konkani was the fertile red mud of their inheritance.)

Augustine waits for judgement. Then Louisa puts him out of his misery: 'That is good. Too many young people do not speak their mother tongues.'

Bertha: Your parents?

Augustine: My father is dead.

Louisa: Please accept our sincere condolences.

Augustine: It happened a while ago.

Louisa: We always regret the loss of a departed parent.

Augustine: Indeed we do.

Louisa: Do you have perpetual Masses sung in his honour?

Augustine: No.

(Augustine was not a believer in a personal god who would listen to your prayers. Even less did he believe that you could pray for someone else. And to have a third party, a disinterested third party, offering intercessory prayers on behalf of people they did not know, seemed outrageous to him. After all, these Masses were subdivided into thousands, since perpetual Mass cards were sold at almost every church in the world and by the minute. There would never be enough priests for even a hundredth of a Mass per soul, and the idea of asking the powers that be to consider minuscule fractions of benefit accruing to the dead seemed far more ridiculous than any other dogmas of the Roman Catholic Church. 'He was a natural Protestant when I met him,' Em would say. 'He protested everything.')

Louisa: Then we shall organize it for you.

Bertha: What's your this-thing?

Augustine: I beg your pardon?

Bertha (impatient): Where do you thissing?

Augustine takes a wild guess and names his parish: Our Lady of Victories.

Bertha nods. Augustine is relieved. He's catching on.

Bertha: You go?

Augustine: I go whenever I am in need of spiritual sustenance.

Louisa would probably have let it go at that. She was a wise woman and she knew that religion was best in small doses. Too much and the boy was no good. There was disquieting evidence in the family itself; their own Cousin Letitia had demonstrated that. Letitia had been the God-fearing woman who went to church every Sunday but she had chosen to live in sin with her Francis. Francis had been willing to marry her in church but it was she who had not wanted marriage. The world knew how often he had asked. The world knew how often they had sex because that was when Letitia would be in the line for confession. The world knew that their first child had been born a bastard. The world knew but did not understand that an atheist-communist-unionist like Francis wanted marriage and a good Catholic girl like Letitia did not. And then they had a son who was a bastard and a son who wasn't. Very often, Louisa's aunt Matilde, Letitia's mother, had said that she would prefer a communist-atheist-unionist like Francis as a child and wondered how her God-fertile womb – a nun and a priest and three angels sent to heaven apart from the five other children – could have borne something as vile and frightening as her last-born with the gentle hands that nursed her in old age and illness. It could get very complicated, this God thing, this love thing.

Bertha knew this too but she did not apply Letitia and her story to their lives. She did not believe in application, so she persisted:

Bertha: How often?

Augustine: Once a year.

Louisa decides that she would have to step in or lose the boy on a technicality.

Louisa: Well, that is between you and your confessor.

Augustine: No, it is between me and God.

On the way home, Louisa was not kind.

'If you do not want your daughter to marry, you should have let me know,' she told Bertha in her most stately Portuguese.

'How can you say that?' Bertha asked.

'Because you were quizzing him on his religion. In these days!'

Bertha protested that she had the right to ask whether her daughter was going to a God-fearing man.

'And how much will you put into your daughter's hands?' Louisa asked savagely. For the matter of dowry had not been discussed. Both sisters had hoped that since this was a love match, there would be no demand made. Both sisters knew that demands were almost inevitable since no Indian wedding was an affair that concerned two people. It took in the family and the family would speak where love would prefer silence. And if a woman did not have any money coming to her, if she was in her late twenties, if she was known to have been 'moving around' with a young man for several years, she had very little bargaining power.

'Here you have a brahmin boy – okay, maybe not a first-class brahmin family, but brahmin, from a good village, with a good job, who wants to marry your daughter . . .'

'Then why . . .'

'He may not have asked. He may need a push or two. Which man doesn't? He earns well. Andrade says he's going to do even better. And you are worried how many times he goes to church? Enough if he goes one more time, at the time of nuptials, that's what I say. But don't ask me, who am I? You know more than I do.'

It was a classic move in the game. If you are older, you can always play this one and sweep the board. Your wisdom has been ignored, your opinions have been spurned with contempt, and you accept this without demur. You know that you have no value in the world. That immediately puts your opposition in the terrible position of having to bring you back into the argument, of having to beg for any further advice; and as soon as an apology is issued, you can put it down for future use. You were slighted. If you were not, why apologize?

After the ladies had left, Augustine simply got on with his work. Perhaps his hand reached for the telephone once. Perhaps he didn't even go so far. He had always had the admirable ability to cut out anything that did not pertain to the problem at hand.

'Can you imagine?' Em said. 'We met that evening and

went out for a Coke float and to the pictures, and he didn't say a word. Though I thought there was a naughty flicker in his eyes and I got ready to ask for his Wassermann report.'

'His what?'

'I didn't even know what it was but Gertie said I should ask for it if he ever asked me to go to a hotel.'

I looked it up; it was a venereal disease test and not even a reliable one at that. It could show that you were carrying syphilis when you were actually suffering from cholera or tuberculosis.

Imelda did not, finally, ask Augustine for his syphilis certificate. But she did continue to be puzzled and a little unnerved by the mischief in his eyes.

She discovered the cause of it later that evening.

I got home and Mae was crying and Tia Madrinha was looking stern and Daddy was reading more intently than usual. When I kissed him, he said, 'Congratulations.' I didn't know what he meant. Then Tia Madrinha said, 'You may ask your young man to ask your father's permission.' Daddy said, with a rare spark, 'Ask my permission when you two went and sought his hand in marriage for my daughter?'

I couldn't believe it. For a moment, I felt such rage, I could have horsewhipped the fatty and her sister.

'How could you do this to me?' I asked. (All right, all right, I screamed.)

'Because we love you,' said Tia Madrinha. 'And tongues are wagging.'

'Whose tongues?'

To which there was of course no reply. But then TM rose like an empress from the throne and said that she was Going

Home. It was clear that she was not. It was clear that she wanted to be made to stay. Darned if I'd do that.

'Thank you so much for calling,' I said.

She misunderstood.

'One day you will indeed thank me for calling on him,' she said. 'But I do not have to reply to you. I shall give witness before God. And *He* will be the best judge of my actions.'

Then Mae started snivelling and I turned on her like a Fury. At this, TM stomped off and then Daddy put down his paper and said, 'For the love of God, Imelda, go and bring that woman back or we shall never hear the end of it.'

So I ate humble pie and brought her back and swallowed my rage because Daddy was looking quite ruffled and I suppose if I have to –

The entry breaks off but begins the next day:

Gertie says that if you say to yourself, 'Every day in every way I get better and better,' you end up getting better. So all morning I told myself, 'I have the chin of that lovely girl in *Anarkali*. And I have the poise of Merle Oberon.' I said it to myself and in the end, when I looked, I still had my own chin. I will never be able to cut an emperor dead at twenty paces in defence of my love as that dancing girl did. And I can't be Merle if I am made to go to church in the morning and confess that I have sinned against my parents and my godmother. So when I called, I don't think I was all cool and ironic. I almost squeaked when I heard his voice on the other end. The usual bark, of course: 'Mendes.' I have tried so hard to modify this but to no avail. And then when I said,

'It's me,' he started to laugh quite immoderately. But something about the stern quality of my silence must have communicated itself so he swallowed his mirth and suggested that we meet for lunch. 'I don't think I could talk about this over lunch,' I say and my tone is edged with a hint of frost. So he says he will spring for tea for two at whatever time I say and at a location to be picked by me. So I say, 'Five thirty at Bombelli's then,' and I hang up.

When I get there, he's already reached. It's five forty-five. He knows he has to give me fifteen minutes of grace because I have to travel into town and he's just a quick hop away, but he's there. He's deep in some specifications. I can tell. I hated specifications when I was at ASL, miles and miles of numbers and if one of them goes wrong, the static won't precipitate or something. I hate them even more just then. My life is in disorder and he's looking at specifications. I feel bruised by the world.

Then he looks up and sees me and his face changes and he comes over and walks me out of the restaurant and to the sea.

(NB: What is it about the sea? Is it because it's there?)

We walked for a bit and then he took my hand and he stopped me and we stood there in the middle of the rush and the push and the chanawallah and the hijras and the laughing babies and gossiping ayahs and the balloons and the clouds and the glitter on the waves turning it all to metal. And then he said, 'Do you want to do this?' I didn't know what to say. Then he said, 'I do.' I thought the girl was supposed to say that. So I did the only thing a fella could do. I nodded. And then he put his hand on the back of my neck. I thought he was going to kiss me in the middle of the rush and the push and the etc. But he just left his hand there and I remember thinking, 'So might a man calm a horse.'

I didn't even know I was crying until he gave me his handkerchief.

Yes, I blubbed. Angela Brazil would have been so ashamed of me but I just couldn't stop blubbing. A policeman came up to us and asked poor LOS what he was up to. LOS said that he was innocent and I had to raise my tear-streaked face and say that I was all right and we were getting married. Only, I seem to have got the tenses wrong so the poor man thought I was saying we were already married. He looked at our hands and I saw that LOS had nice hands. Sort of capable. If we are ever going to have a nuclear bomb fall on us and if we survive, he will be able to build a hut and strangle a huge cockroach. But no rings on those hands. Or on mine.

My parents were taken to the police station.
It must have been an augury of things to come.
Then came another note in the diary. Just two lines:

The two old biddies asked ANDY to introduce them.
Irony of ironies!

'Why?' I asked Em. 'Why was it ironic?'
'Because he was in the running himself for Imelda Carmina Ana . . .' she said and winked. 'Yes, I know. But I was a hot number then even if I didn't know it myself. Now I look at the pictures and I think, "Whoo, she is pretty," but then? I was too busy worrying about whether the cow was eating grass when I got up from my chair. What things women have to worry about! Thank the stars I didn't have to do my

arms and legs. My, I went with Gertie once and she shrieked every time they pulled at the wax.'

'Andrade?' I drew her back to the story.

It began when Audrey said that David had invited her for a drink.

'Who's David?' Imelda had asked.

'Not any old David, silly. *The* David,' Audrey said.

'Which is the David?'

'The one in the movies.'

'You didn't know David?' I asked Em.

'We didn't go and see too many Hindi films. When *Awaara* came out and *Anarkali*, I think, yes, we went for those. And that film about the rickshaw puller which left me so sad for a week, I could hardly eat. But not so many that I would know who David was. But Audrey said that she was keen to meet him. I said she should go then. But she said, all girly-girly, that she couldn't possibly unless I went along. So I shrugged my shoulders and said I would go. We met in a nice quiet little place which seemed to have been done up to look like a European restaurant. You know, fat candles, white-and-red-checked tablecloths, brave chrysanthemums and a girl in peach satin singing the blues. Only the waiters were Indian and one of them was picking his nose. He saw me look and he wiped his hand on the back of the tray. But I suppose they were all boys from the muluk and they didn't know better. I stopped looking at them and focused on the girl singing. She was tapping her cheek with a rosc. I thought that was overdone but she got lots of tips so I suppose it worked so who was I to argue? Audrey and I had got there early, so we just sat there, enjoying it all. What they call ambience these days. I kept thinking, "This is a real restaurant. If anyone took a picture of me now, whoever saw it would know I had been in a real restaurant." Then David arrived. He was a little gnome of a man and seemed friendly. He asked me if I would like something to drink. I said I would like a Coca Cola. "You're a Coca Cola girl, I see," he said. I didn't know what that meant but he said it in a way that suggested it might have many meanings. I was trying to decide whether I was in trouble or not when suddenly Audrey got up and said, "I'm going home," and she left. "What happened?" David asked me. He looked a bit hurt, like a child who has been abandoned on the playground. I should have felt sorry for him. He was bald and gnomey and sad so I said, "Let me go and find out." I thought I could catch up with her. He said, "No, let's just talk. Tell me about yourself, Coca Cola Girl." I thought Audrey might be ill. I began to get worried. I looked at the door. I began to get up. He smiled again and said, "If you leave now, everyone will think I am a naughty man." I sat back down but then he said, "But I *am* a naughty man." In that one second, he changed from a hurt little boy into something greasy.

' "I must freshen up," I said and rose again. He made a grab for my hand. I pulled it away sharply and went to the loo. The singer was in the bathroom. I washed my face and saw that she was looking at me. "You have a nice voice," I said. "Thank you," she said. "And now you walk out of the bathroom and go straight home." I told her I had ordered something. I felt I couldn't leave if I had ordered something. "What did you order?" she asked. "A Coca Cola," I said. "Forget it," she said. "Anyone can drink it. Now you write a little note to him saying that you were ill and had to go home and give it to me." I wrote it and put my name at the end.

"Chhee, chhee, don't sign it, silly. No, better still, I will write it." Then I made such a mistake, I still remember it with shame. I asked, "Doesn't he know your handwriting?" She looked at me for a long moment and then she said, "I *sing* here." Before I could say anything, she added, "And I was trying to help you." I could have wept. "I know," I said, "I'm sorry." I went outside and Andrade was there. He stepped up to me and asked, "What's the matter?" but I couldn't wait to talk. I just wanted to be alone. It was all too much. Audrey wanted to meet David but Audrey ran away. Then David started to act up and so I ran away. Now Andrade was waiting for me and I had to start running. And then Audrey popped out of nowhere and she looked at me. I couldn't take it any more so I started crying. She didn't say anything so I started running. She stopped Andrade from coming after me.'

'But what was that all about?' I asked, confused.

'I asked Audrey the next day but she refused to tell me. It was only when she settled on that sweet-faced Marine who whisked her off to Wisconsin that I got the story out of her. You won't believe this but Andrade wanted to try his chances with me. So he asked her to take me to meet David. He knew David would try something and then he would step in and save me and I would, I suppose, fall over myself in gratitude and fall in love with him.'

'That's . . .'

'Wodehousian? Thought so. But that's what Aud told me.'

'And what was her role in all this?'

'Andy knew I wouldn't go alone so he got her to play along, to say that she wanted to meet David and to take me.'

'But why would she play along?'

'Oh, we all knew she was in love with Andy.'

'She was in love with Andy and so she helped him to get you to try and fall in love with him.'

'The heart has its reasons . . .'

'Yeah, right.'

'I know. I thought it was pretty stupid myself. But when I pushed her she said that she knew it wouldn't work and I would get angry with him and then she would have helped him and she could get a chance.'

'You thought it was a good enough reason for playing along with this kind of shit?'

'I wish you wouldn't use that word.'

'Right, so speaks Miss Clean Mouth.'

'The words I use are always clean.'

'Sure, sure.'

'There are lots of words you can use without evoking images that belong in the toilet and not on the tongue.'

'I think that's the first time I've heard the words toilet and tongue used in the same sentence.'

'Oh? Nothing like that in the Olympia Press?'

'Em!'

'No offence, no offence . . .'

We were wandering again, like lost tourists. I tried bringing her back to the subject of her ambivalence about marriage, but we'd reached a dead end.

Some days later, she showed us a letter to Angel Ears. It filled in some details:

Ever since the day of the inquisition, I have been converted, as if by some alchemy only known to the engaged, the spoken for, into a watering pot. I cry at the least provocation but I am glad to say I do not blub. I simply tear up but only in one eye. Do you find that odd? Do you really want to marry a woman who cries with only one eye?

I know I want to marry you. But I wish we were the first to ever get married. I cannot help feeling that the institution has been somewhat corrupted and corroded by the misuse of others. We could show them, by a beyootiful and myoochooal respect for each other, how things must be conducted.

Have I ever told you how much I love you? Well, darling, I am telling you now, she said and began to drip like a spout.

'You cried a lot when he popped the question?' Susan asked her one day.

'I don't know why I kept crying. Mad things would set me off. Someone would ask me whether I wanted to be a June bride and I would find my face wet. Inside, I was like a monsoon, I was always moist so I didn't know I was crying when I was crying. Once I was sitting in a bus thinking I'd like him to have an engagement ring with a stone the colour of his eyes and I began to cry. A sweet old Muslim woman was sitting next to me. She took my hand and held it for a while. Then she said, *"Duaa kar, beti. Duaa mein badi taaqat hai."* I told her why I was crying, that I was getting married. I must have got the tenses right this time so she asked, *"Nahin karni shaadi?"* I told her I wanted to. *"Bachpan ke liye ro rahi ho,"* she said, smiling. Maybe she was right; maybe I was crying for my childhood. My innocence, if you will.'

Em had suffered migration, displacement and the loss of a home when she was still a girl. After arriving in India, she and her mother had spent some tough months in Calcutta before shifting to Bombay. There they had awaited the arrival of the man of the house, who was still walking from Burma to India through jungles and swamps, surviving malaria and tigers. They had spent those anxious, long months living in a storefront room with no toilet – to use one, they had to walk to a relative's house once a day. And when she grew up Em had had to give up her studies and work to support the family. She'd been doing it for over a dozen years. And yet marriage felt like growing up? It seemed odd to me.

There's also Granny's version. She confirmed that Em had been angry – 'She was very thissing' – but that it hadn't lasted more than a few hours, as Granny had known it wouldn't, because which girl wouldn't want a man with perfect manners and a good salary and even better prospects? And a brahmin, too. Granny said she did not need to ask him about being a brahmin. She claimed that she knew.

'A brahmin boy but a poor one,' was how she described him, once we got past her elisions.

'How could you know he was poor?'

Here Granny squared her shoulders and jerked her chest out.

'He had a good body?'

'Worker's body,' she said. Then she spread out her hands and curved them so that they were slightly like claws.

'Big hands?' I ventured.

She nodded.

'And his eyes,' she said, as if that set a seal on things.

My mother's eyes: amber.

My father's eyes: blue.

I didn't think it could be that easy. If blue eyes were a

sign of aristocracy, it couldn't have been a local aristocracy. Indian eyes are dark brown, shading sometimes to black. Blue eyes, green eyes, brown eyes were always suspicious, even if they are fetishized now. It was common in my childhood to call people who had them 'cat-eyed'. It was also common to say that they could not be trusted, that they were 'double-faced'. The suspicion clearly arises out of the belief that where there are signs of the European face, there must be strains of the European gene pool. In other words, a honky in the woodpile. But what would the honky find in the woodpile in Goa? Surely, not women of the privileged elite, of the compradors? Surely, those genes would have found their way into the lower castes where the men of the family were less empowered, where droit du seigneur might still be a practice? It was no use telling Granny this. She would have been horrified at the thought.

'It was good we went,' said Granny, 'because otherwise they would still be this-thing and you two would not thissing.' They would still have been visiting bookshops, she meant, and Susan and I would not have been born.

'Nonsense,' said The Big Hoom when we suggested that he had been coerced to the altar by two old ladies in silky frocks. 'It was on my mind. I would have asked.'

'Gosh,' said Em when we told her this. 'I wonder how I would have answered if I had been asked. The standard response was the Hollywood one. You know, you said you had no idea, this was such a surprise, you were very honoured, could have some time to think about it? This meant 'Yes'. But if you were going to say 'No', you had to say it immediately while *not* saying 'No'. You had to say you had no idea, this had come as a surprise, could you have some time to think about it?'

'That's the same thing,' I pointed out.

'It is but a sensible man knows.'

I thought this didn't actually work but I didn't say so.

Em spotted it in my face.

'You don't think so?'

'I think,' I said carefully, 'that we can never be sure what we are communicating.'

'Oh go on, wise boy. I think men know. Women certainly know.'

I shrugged. 'We were talking about your engagement. You were angry with them.'

'I don't know if opposition would have worked. It's difficult to remember who I was, baba. You have no idea how odd it seems to read my diary now. Who *was* that girl? What a fey, frightened creature! What a frigging woodland nymph! Maybe I would have been happy that someone had forced the issue. I was twenty-eight going on frigid. I didn't think much of the sex act . . .'

'Oh God, here we go.'

'No, really. It seemed very messy and painful. Audrey had told me all about her first night. So I was very happy to be kissed from time to time, to have my hand held on Marine Drive, to know there was someone to squire me about. I don't think I wanted more. Or did I? I mean, I knew I wanted to marry him but not then. And then there was all the bother of children. We would have to have them once we married, of course. That kind of thing.'

'Ambivalence,' I said wisely.

'Ambivalence? I love it. I was ambivalent. I think I am

ambivalent right now. I think I am an ambivalence, toon taan toon taan toon taan, with a blue light on my forehead. So which side would have won? Would I have simpered off into a corner and said, "Whatever you want for me, Mum and Tia Madrinha" or would I have said "You go there and I'll run away and join a convent"? I don't know.'

'They might have taken that very seriously.'

'Of course they would. I wanted to be a nun, they knew that. Only, I didn't want to sleep alone in a room. I would have been very lonely. No, I'm lying. I would have been scared. But Mother Catherine said that nuns had to sleep alone in their cells. I think they must be worried about lesbianism. She said that Jesus would be there to look after me. I didn't believe her. I wasn't taking risks with that fellow. I mean, "Thy will be done"? What if it was his will that I be terrified every night for the rest of my life? I much prefer his mother. She just says "Pray to me", which I can understand. He's far too demanding. What's all this —"I surrender all, I surrender all"? Is that a hymn to sing? For a woman? I sang that once and he took away the hearing in my left ear. I thought, "Well, bloody hell, enough of you lot. I'm not surrendering anything."'

'Did it leave a God-sized hole in your life?'

'That sounds suspiciously like a quotation,' she said. 'I wish you wouldn't. I never feel like I'm having a conversation with someone who quotes.'

She looked at me, a cold, hard stare.

'It is a quote, isn't it?'

'It feels like one.'

'I hate quotes,' she said fiercely. 'I feel like I'm talking to a book. I feel like I'm talking to history. I feel like I'm being practised upon.'

'Practised upon?'

'For a public performance. For a debate club. For some schoolboy shit like that.'

She refused to be drawn any further and stomped off for a beedi.

The next time she talked about the courtship and engagement, some of the details had changed a little. I could spot some contradictions. But the script was the same, and she insisted that she had wanted to be a nun. She had wanted 'none of this'.

'You didn't want to get married?' I asked.

'Who wants to get married?' Em asked rhetorically. 'Only those who want children.'

'You didn't want children?' I don't remember who said this, Susan or I or both of us together.

'Oh God, no. I saw what children do. They turn a good respectable woman into a mudd-dha. I didn't want to be a mudh-dha. I didn't want to be turned inside out. I didn't want to have my world shifted so that I was no longer the centre of it. This is what you have to be careful about, Lao-Tsu. It never happens to men. They just sow the seed and hand out the cigars when you've pushed a football through your vadge. For the next hundred years of your life, you're stuck with being someone whose definition isn't even herself. You're now someone's *mudd-dha*!'

She suddenly realized who she was talking to.

'Of course, when it happens, you don't regret it and all that shit, okay?'

She grinned, a silty grin. 'You were my two dividends, yes? Don't you forget that.'

Then she sighed, took a deep breath, and said, 'But what an investment. My life.'

We didn't say much. We weren't allowed. We held our peace and tried to work with what we'd been given. We tried to reassure ourselves that honesty was the best policy in the long run and that we would be glad, eventually, that we knew what Em thought.

Or that's what I tell myself.

7.

'The Disgusting Bitch'

We never knew when the weather would change dramatically with Em. You're vulnerable to those you love and they acknowledge this by being gentle with you, but with Em you could never be sure whether she was going to handle you as if you were made of glass or take your innermost self into a headlock. Sometimes it seemed part of her mental problem. Sometimes it seemed part of her personality. 'That's not her, it's her problem,' Susan once said to me, when she found me weeping because of something Em had said. It became a way of escaping the sharpness of her tongue. But it also became a way of escaping her as a person. We could always dismiss what she was saying as an emanation of the madness, not an insult or a hurt or a real critique to be taken seriously. We often did dismiss what she said, but more often than not, it was self-defence.

And there were times when all defences failed.

I come home from a bad day at my first job. I'm twenty and I've been assigned a story. At my position on the totem pole, the story is not about what I think of the issues involved, it is about what other people think. My job is to make them think aloud and put it all down on paper, and to that end, I must call and ask them for their time. But no one is available. One is out of town and nobody knows how he can be reached. The next is not at home and when I call his office he's 'not on his seat'. The secretary of a third appears to have put his phone permanently off the hook. I call and call and all the time I'm aware that there's a whole beast of a machine waiting for copy. The desk, the designers, the editor, all looking at you as if you're shirking if you stop calling even for a minute. I need quotes and the only quote I've managed to get is from the B-List, an add-on remark which is not without value but only when the experts from the A-List, the politicians, the CEOs, the film stars, have spoken. And none of them have.

When I'm home, I'm hoping to set it all down, though I know failure is never shed so easily. Victories evanesce quickly enough. Failure hangs around you like a cloak and everyone is kind and pretends not to see it.

Not Em.

She wades into the thick of it.

'Bad day at the office? I can smell it on you. Now *there's* a man beaten by the system I would say to the bishop, if there were a bishop sitting next to me. But this ain't no bishop, this is my son and he's no great big ball of gas today. Give us a hug.'

I give her a hug. She reeks of beedi smoke and hair oil and Iodex.

'You in pain?'

'Pain pain go away, come again some other day. Little Johnny wants to play with himself.'

I don't want a nasty riff on nursery rhyme. I want tea and sympathy.

'I asked you a question.'

'No, you did not. You made a statement.'

'Okay, let's go back a bit. Are you in pain?'

She strikes a pose, her wrist to her forehead. 'You cannot imagine the torment.'

Then she peers at me.

'No pain, no. I just ate some Iodex.'

I don't know how to respond. She could be joking.

'Open your mouth.'

'Ha ha ha,' she mocks. But her mouth is open and at the back, I can see a black smear. I reach in with a finger and dab at it. I sniff. Iodex.

'Why?'

'Because the sky is so high and the crow shat in your left eye. I could tell you a lie but I don't see why. The world is a game and the game is a tie. The tie is around your neck and they'll string you high.'

There were times when I could see a lot of my mother in the body whom I met at home. There were times when there was very little of her. This was one of those times. She was a parody of herself. The mania had taken over but it was a sly episode. She was sitting there, smoking as if she were ordinarily manic. Whatever that means. But she wasn't. She was into pica, the desire to eat extraordinary stuff, and that was unprecedented. She was suggesting my death and that was also something she wouldn't normally do. I wanted to reach out to her, even though I knew from previous experience that this was futile. I wanted to understand her and her predicament because I was her son and I loved her with a helpless corroded love. I wanted to but I could only shout.

'What the fuck are you talking about? Why can't you answer straight, you piece of shit?'

Em opened her eyes wide. I looked into my own eyes.

'You're angry. Ooh, my little p'ecious boy is angry. He's angry. I'm frightened.'

The mockery was apparent and hideous – she mimed trembling – but it reminded me that this was part of her illness. I tried to calm down.

'I've had a tough day at work . . .'

'Ooh, he's had a tough day at work. And for what? For some three thousand rupees. Can't buy much with three thousand rupees. Can't go far with three thousand rupees. Can't even live on his own with three thousand rupees.'

I could not remember ever feeling so violated and hurt.

'Shut up,' I said and I could hear my voice beginning to tremble with tears. 'Shut up, you disgusting bitch.'

'Do you want a cuppa?' she asked, suddenly herself.

'Are you fucking mad?' I was almost beside myself.

'Shhh,' she said and suddenly picked up the book in which she wrote letters to people, letters that never got posted unless Susan read them and decided that they would not hurt the recipients.

'They're listening.'

'Who?'

She rolled her eyes and looked desperate.

'Who?' I asked again. 'Who's listening?'

Now her expression suggested that she had transcended despair. Now she was willing to play some mad endgame which she thought I had inaugurated.

'It began when you were a baby. You pointed to the fan and I knew that they were there, that they were listening. You found them first.'

'Are they listening now?'

She rolled her eyes again and then, as if she couldn't bear

the whole thing, the stupidity of her son, the pressure of the performance, she shouted, 'Go, then. Go. Do your damnedest. But if you touch one hair on my family's head, you'll regret it.'

Then she smiled and said, 'Can the disgusting bitch make you some tea? You must be tired.'

The next morning I found a note under my pillow.

I have to get you all out of here. If they come for us, they must not get us all. I have to drive you out. You have to go. That's why I said what I said. I'm very proud of you but they must not know. If they think I hate you, they may spare you. Go. Go away. Himself and I can manage. We'll go down together, in flames. We can take it. We've lived and loved. You haven't. I want you to live and love but when you do, they can get you. Susan, they can't touch, she's pure of heart. She can stay. But you must go. Soon. But wait for my birthday. And get me a Cadbury's chocolate. Cad equals Catholic. Bury all the Catholics. Don't tell anyone.

The note was signed 'The Disgusting Bitch'.

I didn't know what to make of it. Em was asleep and so we were all very quiet that morning. I went to work and tried hard not to consider all the issues that were unresolved. When I got home, Em was gone. She had been hospitalized again, at her own suggestion. Susan was with her and The Big Hoom was taking a nap, probably worn out by the hospital thing. When we had dinner together, I suggested to The Big Hoom that I move out. He continued eating quietly as he thought about it. Then he looked at me carefully.

'It might be a good idea,' he said. 'Can you afford it?'

'No,' I replied.

He smiled, but it was brief and as much grimace as smile. Then he said, 'Then the question doesn't arise, does it?'

'But you're not opposed to the idea?'

He put down his spoon and looked at me steadily. He said, 'You will always be welcome to live here. It is your home as much as it is anyone else's. But if you want to move, do it when you can, not when you want to.'

As a prescription, that wasn't a bad one: when you can, not when you want to.

When I went to visit Em in hospital, her eyes were aquaria, full of strange living forms and artificial additions. She had finished cleaning the lady in the next bed who kept spitting up her food. But she was not yet completely there.

'I hear the words of a song and the music of another. They play together like children. Like children entering the kingdom of heaven. How much chocolate can there be in heaven? The food of the Gods and the shit of the Gods. For me, the food. For Mae, the shit. She wants her gold back, poor darling. I wonder when it went. Where it went. How it went. Why it went, we know. Why, Sister Sarah, why? What it went does not work. Do you follow me?'

She was free associating, gliding through language.

'I follow.'

'Oh no, you don't. Following me will bring you here and here is where the mad people are. You don't have to be mad. I went mad so that you don't have to be. You don't have to do anything now that I am the disgusting bitch.'

'I didn't mean that.'

'What?'

I looked at her carefully. She was not letting me see what

she was thinking. So I knew, immediately, that she had registered the thoughtless insult and that it had mattered. She was not going to give me proof so there was no way I could actually apologize. But I tried.

'I'm sorry I said that.'

'Sorry, sorry, kiss the lorry, the schoolboys would say. There was one who walked down the road shouting, "Tony Greig, lambu-ta!" And there was another who read me a poem about butterflies. He read it under the mango tree while I waited for you.'

There was no going in. And there was no going away. I pushed my chair back from her bed, closer to the window with three vertical iron bars, and went back to the book I had carried with me. I read through Em's rhymes about mango trees and her Mae and Satan's bee. I read till she was tired and only mumbling, and then The Big Hoom came and I could go home.

In my late teens, prey to all kinds of inadequacies, I embarked on a programme of remedial reading. First, Plato, an omnibus edition with forty-eight of the fifty-five dialogues, which left me annoyed and exhausted because I did not believe that beauty had much to do with truth or vice versa. And then, for no apparent reason, I began reading the *Mahabharata* in Kamala Subramaniam's translation. This was wild and terrifying and it almost drove me to despair. The whole book seemed to be a thicket of names and relationships, many of which sounded dangerously like each other. I used a piece of paper, solemnly writing down the names of the Pandavas, their antecedents, their wife and wives and children and relatives, but it was still difficult. Finally, I grew exhausted – it was summer, the hardcover edition was cutting into my chest, and the sun was bright outside – and so I began reading from page to page, not bothering about who was who. Once I had given up trying to conquer the text, it began to glow with an epic excess of almost every conceivable human passion. I was transfixed.

Then I came upon the Bhagawad Gita and it seemed as if Krishna was speaking to me. He was telling me that if I were a student then I had to be a student. I did not have to be my mother's nurse. I had to do my duty according to my station in life . . .

For a whole six hours one morning, I felt the glow of a benign blue Hinduism pouring down upon me. At the end of that period, I looked across the room. Em loved the heat, so she had had a good summer, full of manic energy and insomnia. She had been on a roll, talking endlessly, making or asking for endless cups of tea, roaring at all of us if we asked for peace and quiet. 'You'll get an eternity of peace and quiet in the grave.' She would sober down a little only when The Big Hoom returned from work in the evenings, but when he was in the kitchen, cooking, she would break loose.

April had been quieter, but then Em was a great respecter of education. When we were studying for examinations, she could always be quelled by one of us saying, sounding agonized, 'I'm studying.' 'Okay, then I'll zip my lip,' she would say and light another beedi and scratch out a letter to someone. Or make some more tea. Perhaps the processes calmed her, though there was nothing Zen-like or ceremonial about the way she made tea, whistling old snatches of Broadway and vaudeville melodies as she thumped and slammed and poured and strained and sugared and slurped her way through another cup, standing up, her head already bubbling over with something else that had to be said.

But this was well into June. Susan and I hadn't had any need to study for over a month; there had been nothing to restrain Em. She had exhausted herself and us with her mania. And now, as I put away the *Mahabharata*, I knew instantly that she was beginning the slide into depression. Perhaps it was the silence that had disturbed me and broken the spell of the Blue God's arguments.

Em had lit a beedi but she was staring at the floor, as if it might conceal a pattern or a story.

After a few seconds, she shook her head like a dog pestered by a fly, got up, stretched and said, 'Time for another cuppa.'

'I'll join you if I may,' I said.

'No hope of *my* joining you while *you* make it, is there?' she said. 'No, I thought not.' Then she was in the kitchen, silent, and the slow sounds of the pan being put on the stove, the tins being opened, her feet dragging across the cramped space told me that she was sinking into night, that the black drip had started inside her.

I could hold on to my karma defence for a little longer but it was already seeming thin. How could you do your duty when love beckoned you to do something else? No, that was easy enough. Lord Krishna had dealt with that: you ignored love.

And I tried to. When Em was 'high', I could be a busy student, in every sense of the word. I could run amok in art galleries where I would write comments and sign them as John Ruskin or Clement Greenberg. I could watch two long movies back-to-back at film festivals. I could spend entire afternoons borrowing and returning books from three libraries in three different parts of the city. I could find fifty other ways to block her out because she could be an extremely painful mother for an adolescent boy.

On an ordinary day, returning from college, I would be greeted with: 'Hey sexy, did you have any luck today?'

'Luck?'

'Did you get any sex?'

'Em!'

'So you didn't. Those girls must be blind.'

'Stop it.'

'But maybe it's all to the good. When Susan was born, Griselda came over. You remember Griselda, no? She was with me at the AmConGen . . . She had beautiful boobs. I think she was a forty but I couldn't be sure. I shouldn't have been looking, do you think? I mean, was it a bit lesbian? I looked but I don't think I wanted to touch. You know when I found your *Debonair* . . .'

'You what?'

'Oh, I put it back, don't worry. Behind the tank in the toilet, what a place! I suppose you'd have hidden them under the mattress in your room, if you had a room. Poor beetle, where else are you going to fiddle?'

'Em!'

'Anyway, I looked at the centrefolds and I thought, some nice girls. But I didn't want to nuzzle.'

'Em!'

Her conversation had a way of reducing me to exclamations. I think she enjoyed that and worked out exactly how she was going to do it.

'O Lord, talk won't make tea, will it? Let me get you a cup that cheers but does not inebriate and a biscuit and we'll be convivial.'

The phone rang.

'Do you want to come and see *Wada Chirebandi*? There's a couple of spare tickets.'

I did.

I finished my tea, raced through a bath and was out and confronting this new world of plays and texts and poetry readings. There was always something to do and in my haste to get away from home, I was always willing to make up the numbers. I didn't really care what it was: *Man of Marble* by Wajda, a dance performance by a young bharatanatyam exponent, an experimental play in Gujarati in which somewhat sheepish young men walked past the action, dressed in black masks with tyres balanced on their narrow shoulders. Much of it was ridiculous, but there were also moments that were sublime and among them I discovered what art could do.

Mahesh Elkunchwar's *Wada Chirebandi* turned out to be one of those moments. It outlined a fairly simple story: a traditional upper-caste family, three brothers, one in the city, one on the farm, and Chandu. Where did Chandu fit in? Chandu was the young man who looked after the matriarch of the family played by an asthmatic and self-pitying wheeze emanating off-stage. Chandu had no life other than her. Chandu tore me from my Blue God Defence. What if my karma were to stop and wait? What if each time I blocked my ears to Em's desperate muttering I was denying what I was supposed to be doing? And of course, I could see it was the humanitarian thing to do: to sit by your mother's bed and hold her hand and see if one could reach her.

'You can't reach her,' Dr Marfatia, who was then her psychiatrist, had said once as Em was led away by hands that were firm and gentle. Or at least hands we hoped were gentle. 'How do we know they don't hurt her?' I had asked The Big Hoom, and he had said, 'Because she never protests when she has to go to Ward 33. That is all we'll know. We'll have to live with that much.' And she had gone willingly into the hospital one more time, releasing us, returning us to ourselves. 'Go, live.' Did she say this to me when she was led away that time, or am I imagining it?

Except that none of the three she left behind knew *how* to go and live; we didn't know what to do with the brief freedom because it was a tainted freedom. And each time Em came home, we all hoped, for a little while, that the pieces of the jigsaw would fall into place again. Now we could be a textbook illustration: father, mother, sister, brother. Four Mendeses, somewhat love-battered, still standing.

Barely standing, and that wasn't enough. Home was where others had to gather grace. Home was what I wanted to flee.

Home was a blood-stained bathroom which, when it was scraped down for repainting, revealed an old suicide note, scrawled in pencil. So the one I remembered, the one Susan and I had witnessed, that one was attempt number three, at the very least.

Home was uncertainty: Who would open the door? Em in a panic of sorrow? Em in a rage against some unnamed enemies? Em in a laughing fit with a beedi fuming in her hands?

One day, under the huge mango tree that stood in the schoolyard, with a bunch of schoolboys standing around me, mocking me for being the son of a mad woman, I thought suddenly and automatically: 'I want to go home.' And then I thought as suddenly: 'I don't want to go home.' I remember thinking, 'If I go on like this, I will go mad.' I tried not to think too much about home as a concept after that.

Inside and outside, inside and outside. Each exerted its own special pull on me. My job as a journalist meant late nights; you did not leave the office until the newspaper was put to bed. This meant I was away until ten-thirty on most days; Susan, as a lecturer in English literature at a college, came home by mid-afternoon. I would call her soon after and ask, 'Everything okay?' This was code for 'Is she all right?' Her reply would always be, 'About the same,' but this was as false as it was true. Em was subject to microweathers; her manic phase could vary from cheerful and laughing to malevolent and sneering, and back again within an hour. In contrast, her depressive phases were almost unrelieved in their darkness. Susan was a stoic; she would bear with Em and she would never complain but that made it all the more difficult to bear. Had she whined about taking the brunt of these blasts, I might have escaped into the office with an easier conscience.

Work was a great thing. I could bring it home and shore it up against Em's importuning. As a cultural journalist, I could claim that the new play, the old film, the experimental poetry reading, the script session – all these fell within my purview and required my presence.

'Off again?' Em would ask.

'Off again,' I would say.

And through all this, I told myself, and with all this, I told myself, I'll try and understand her. I'll try and figure out how this happened to my mother, once a beautiful woman with a lovely singing voice, and – yes – how this happened to my father, a man with a future who had given it all up to make sure the present was manageable. For her. For us.

8.

'Three to get married'

The engagement was low-key. This was all to the good because Imelda had thrown another fit when she saw the engagement ring she was supposed to present to her fiancé. And the battle did not die there. It went on for years afterwards. We would hear it from time to time as Em and Granny repeated the old lines.

Em: I wanted a blue stone to match his eyes. What I got was the tiniest chip of sapphire.

Granny: All we could thissing [afford].

Em: Who asked you for a sapphire?

Granny: Who said thissing [blue stone]?

Em: Yes, but is there only one blue stone in the world?

Granny: You're saying we should have given a semi-thissing [semi-precious stone]?

Em: That is precisely what I'm suggesting.

Granny: We don't do that-thing.

It puzzled me, this ability to fight over things that had happened years ago until I realized that Em and Granny could only fight over things that had happened years ago. They used them as placeholders for the slights and hurts of the present. In ten years time, whatever was bothering them now would spill out into the open, when it could be handled just that much better.

'It's a stupid argument,' said The Big Hoom from behind his newspaper one convivial Sunday afternoon. Granny had just left, muttering about thankless children, and we were having a rare family moment over cups of Nescafé and under a pall of beedi smoke.

'I liked the ring.'

'You wore it on the wrong side, with the flake pointing inwards,' Em said.

'I didn't say I thought it was a good-looking ring. I said I liked it.'

'How can you like an ugly ring?'

He put down the paper and focused his attention on her.

'It came from you.'

Em melted but tried to look unmoved. The paper went back up.

'Did you continue visiting bookshops after the engagement?' I asked.

'No time,' said The Big Hoom.

'Don't you ever marry anyone,' said Em feelingly. 'You cannot do that to a woman you love. Once you've said yes and the family knows that it's on, an invisible machine forms around you. It's here, it's there, it's everywhere. No one is outside its workings. Nothing you do is exempt. It takes all your time, every waking minute. I suppose it's all right if you're not working, but if you are, then it's curtains to everything else. Your evenings are full. You have to go and choose the lace. You choose it. Then someone tells your mother, Have you looked at the lace at this other shop, it might be better. But we've already bought the lace, you say. No, your mother says, this is your wedding, we can return that lace if we get a better lace at the same price, that's what the man said. No, you say, he was only making a sales pitch, there's no point going, he won't take it back. But Mae is a literalist when she wants to be, so we have to go and see more lace. And we have to stop by at Dodo's . . .'

'Who's Dodo?' Susan asked.

'Oh God, can the world have changed so swiftly? Can the world have forgotten Dodo of Clare Road?'

'The world may well have not. I just don't know who you're talking about.'

'You're a literalist too. Me, I believe in metaphors.'

'Never mind the metaphors. Who was Dodo?'

Dodo, apparently, made every wedding dress in Saint Anne's. She heard about engagements even before they were announced.

'About two days after Angel Ears came and asked for my hand, she was there, with swatches of lace and pieces of satin and pattern books and photographs of bouquets and godknowswhat.'

'A pushy broad.'

'She was a single woman living on her own, with an only son, Christopher, and our family stole that son from her.'

'Yes, yes, Sarah-Mae the nurse.'

'You know that story?' Em looked at Susan, surprised.

'Who doesn't?'

'She had a good idea, Sarah-Mae. Find a nice, meek boy and run around with him for as long as you want.'

'I don't think it ended quite so well. He ran off to Canada with her money or something, no?'

'Yes, but at least she didn't have to wander about the city

with her mother distributing wedding cards to people she barely knew.'

'Did The Big Hoom also do it?'

'Did you?'

The newspaper rustled.

'No,' he said briefly.

Susan tapped on the newsprint barrier. The Big Hoom relented and offered an explanation: 'I thought, those who want to come will come and those who don't, won't. So why bother?'

'Didn't you even tell your friends?'

'They knew before the cards were printed. Only the details were needed and those were on the cards, which could be sent by post.'

I thought this made sense. 'That sounds like a solution. Why didn't you do that?' I asked Em.

'Well, I wasn't as smart as Hizzonner. I didn't know that was something I could do because I didn't know that was what he had done. I only found out on the honeymoon.'

Em stopped talking. Susan and I tensed. 'Honeymoon' could set her off, and we feared it might be something we would rather not hear. Not with The Big Hoom around, not when she was having a 'normal' day and there would be nothing to hide behind.

Em began. 'I won't do it on the first night, I told him. I was thinking of poor Audrey. She had screamed fit to bring the house down, she said. The hotel people had to come and stop things. I was dying of shame and pain for her as she told me all this, but when I saw her face she looked as pleased and proud as if she'd been mentioned in *Punch*!'

Susan and I squirmed. The Big Hoom was silent. Em,

thankfully, fell silent too. Susan shot up to clear the table. On her way to the kitchen, she switched on the radio.

One day I found a pair of letters in an envelope marked 'Contract'.

Dear Angel Ears,

I know we have agreed to pledge our troth & etc. And this may come as a shock but it is best said now before it is too late and you discover the awful truth for yourself and end up hurt and miserable and believing that you have been cheated.

Without further roundaboutation, then.

(She takes a long steadying draught of tasteless tea. Just so you should know how difficult this is to write.)

I do not think I am much interested in the whole business of copulation. I love you deeply and I enjoy very much our 'necking and petting'. I must say I thought it pretty disgusting that one should open one's mouth but I closed my eyes and prayed to Saint Anne and that seemed to work and now I'm quite accustomed to the taste of it. I may even have developed a taste for it, which, I suppose, I might attribute to the magic of love.

But from what I have read – and I must say that Three to Get Married was not very explicit on the subject and, despite all the fierce warnings from the pulpit, nor was Alberto Moravia – it seems as if the whole penetration thing might be more fun for you than for me.

Please read this letter seriously. I can almost imagine you smiling here. I feel warm thinking about your smile, but you must not imagine me smiling. You must imagine that my eyes are meeting yours directly and I am refusing to smile. (I am the greatest hypocri-sissy in the world.)

So: what if I don't take to the thing? How often will you expect it? Will I be within my rights to refuse? I asked Father Fabregad but he said, 'That will settle itself by and by,' and went all twinkly and rosy and Portugoosey on me. Though why I should ask a celibate man what a woman's rights are, beats even me. But who else, I wondered, and that's when I thought, well, there's him to whom . . . He's the most concerned in this affair, after all.

I will never speak to you again if you mention this letter to me or if you do not reply in full and with frankness.

With all that my mind and spirit can muster,

Imelda

Only recently, after some years of an on-again-off-again search, I found a second-hand copy of *Three to Get Married*. It's a book by Fulton Sheen, now Servant of God. Written in the beautifully expressive prose of the pulpit, it is quite clear about certain things:

> If love does not climb, it falls. If, like the flame, it does not burn upward to the sun, it burns downward to destroy. If sex does not mount to heaven, it descends into hell. There is no such thing as giving the body without giving the soul. Those who think they can be faithful in soul to one another, but unfaithful in body, forget that the two are inseparable. Sex in isolation from personality does not exist! An arm living and gesticulating apart from the living organism is an impossibility. Man has no organic functions isolated from his soul.

It's easy to mock. No organic functions isolated from the soul? You fart and your soul knows what you ate at the last meal? Your hair falls and your soul clucks its tongue over your failure to use conditioner after a shampoo? And the book never mentions the genitals at all. Nor does it mention the word orgasm. It is an abstract work as befits the idea of a man, a woman and a god getting married; it is full of paradoxes which stop short of the Chestertonian. Yet, it was the book that was given to almost every affianced couple of the Roman Catholic persuasion, and it had a lasting effect on many.

Thirty years after Em was a teenager, we were being told the story of the Pieta in school by the Father Henrys and the Sister Marias: Michelangelo was asked why his Virgin was so young and beautiful even as she held the broken body of her thirty-three-year-old son in her arms. And he is supposed to have said: 'Do you not know that chaste women stay fresh much more than those who are not chaste? How much more in the case of the Virgin, who had never experienced the least lascivious desire that might change her body?' Even in the 1980s, when I entered the 'dangerous' period in which I might violate the temple of the Lord, Sin was about sex; Sanctity was about chastity. Imelda must have been prey to far greater fears and shame in her youth. It is a small miracle that she wrote Augustine the kind of letter she did.

But the reply she received had all the hallmarks of the man who became The Big Hoom. He got straight to the point and got past it.

Dear Imelda,

In accordance with your wishes, I did not imagine you smiling. I did not smile myself.

But I am willing to take my chances.

Your body is yours to give or not. Should you decide not, I will respect that, although I must warn you that I will work hard to reverse your decision.

Let me say, though, that I find all the signs most encouraging. Shall we go forward then?

Love,
Augustine.

I showed Em the letters. She read them both and began to cry, but only out of one eye. ('I gave up crying from both eyes after Vietnam,' she said, and meant it.)

'It was the first time,' she said after a bit, 'that I knew there was an alternative. And only after that, I knew how scared I was of the whole sex thing. We had been told it was the gateway to hell, that we would lose everything if we went all the way. We were told that men were dangerous. Unpredictable. Violent. You could never be sure what would happen if you were alone with them. They could not be relied on if they had had something to drink. A girl had to be ready for anything. Then, as soon as you were all ready to get married, the same people told you: close the door and be his wife.'

'Have sex with him, you mean.'

'That was only one part of it. In those days, it wasn't even a problem if he gave you a slap or two. Everyone gets a couple, they'd say. They don't know their own strength, that's why he broke your jaw, how else is he to make sure you respect him, what else can a man do . . .'

She stopped. Perhaps she saw something on my face.

'No, no, not him. He never did. Though God knows I gave him enough cause. Do you remember Black Pants?'

9.

'You won't do anything silly?'

'Black Pants?'

'You should remember. You were there.'

'I was where?'

'No, maybe you were too little. It was the time that the fan was sending messages.'

The fan had been sending messages for a while. Often, these were innocuous messages that had very little impact on the family. The fan – or the people in the fan, we were never sure since the singular and the plural were both used – might dictate a jam sandwich to be consumed at three o'clock in the morning or the washing of the curtains a few days after they had been hung. But this time, the message was clear. Take your son and leave the house.

She did.

'I think it was some time in the afternoon. You didn't want to go but you came anyway because in those days you followed me around with a sad look in your eyes. Did I ever tell you that you broke my heart?'

'Repeatedly.'

'I hope you carry some guilt around.'

'You must stop reading those American magazines.'

'Who brings them home in the first place?'

Mother and son wander out on to the road. For a moment,

Em seems uncertain about which way she should turn but she knows she will have to move quickly or the friendly neighbourhood watch that keeps an eye on her, an informal eye out for her or for her children, will be alerted. When she begins to walk, she's sure. This is the path they intend her to take. She knows almost every time she takes a wrong turn that she's going the wrong way. The boy tires quickly since he has been promised nothing. There is no treat, no film, no circus, no cream cake, no friendly aunt, nothing at the end of this endless walk in the sun.

And he is barefoot.

'Black Pants pointed it out to me.'

Black Pants stops the woman and the child and asks, 'Where are his shoes?'

'Shoes?' Em asks.

'The boy. He will get blisters.'

Em looks down. The boy is accustomed to being barefoot. His mother has never seen the point of footwear and has let him run around rough. But it is hot today and the ground beneath his feet has begun to sear through his tough soles, and he is hopping from foot to foot.

'I will carry him,' says Black Pants and picks the boy up. The boy whines and squirms and twists and pulls at his own hair and knuckles his eyes. He is accustomed to this being enough. He gets his way with this much.

'I took you from him though you were too big for anyone to carry. But the voices were still there. They were shouting now. I could not make out what they were saying. It was all very confusing and in the middle of it, I found us in a restaurant and Black Pants was having tea and you were crying, a-haan, a-haan, a-haan. I didn't know what to do. I wanted to go home. But I had ordered something. I don't know what. I didn't have money. An ice cream came for you. You refused it. I knew then that it was poisoned and they had come for you.'

The woman is now thoroughly confused. The voices are not so loud now but they have decided that she must pay for not listening attentively enough. Now, they speak in one voice but they speak in code. 'Fate is a sea without shore,' they say. 'Love and Death have dealt shocks,' they say. 'How did you come to eat your ring finger in a sandwich?' they ask. Sometimes they sing. They sing fragments of hymns and Hindi film songs. She knows they are Hindi film songs because she knows the tunes; she does not know the words. There are times when she believes that she might be able to help everyone if she knew the words.

'Yes, I know Hindi,' the man is saying.

'I can teach you Hindi in one hour,' the man says.

'But I am leaving town tomorrow,' the man says.

'He can play as we learn,' the man says.

'I have a room nearby,' the man says.

She does not want to go. The voices are very quiet now. They are watching her very carefully. This will decide what will happen next. They have never done this before. They have always been clear about what they thought, who should be in the papers the next morning, what she can no longer say. The terrifying thing about them is that, today, she can't tell what mood they are in. She can't tell anything except that she knows now that Black Pants wants to have sex with her. As they walk, he is touching her wherever he can.

'Is this what you want?' she asks them aloud. 'Is this what it will take?'

There is no answer. Just a whispering. No, not even whispering; they're rustling, like satin handkerchiefs left too long in a box.

Black Pants is urging her on faster as if he has caught some of her anxieties, her ambivalences.

'Forgive me,' she says to her husband, in her head. She thinks of him and something warm breaks through her eyelids. She is crying, from both eyes. Her son notices. He screams now, screams and vomits. This is not an ordinary child's crying but the sound of a child in despair. She sets him down to speak to him but immediately a crowd has gathered. The boy is struggling with her, trying to hit her because he is now on the verge of hysterics. The man tries to intervene. The boy's screams become shrieks. In this city, every deserted street corner conceals a crowd. It appears in a minute when something disrupts the way in which the world is wont to work. It can disappear almost as instantaneously.

The crowd sizes up the situation immediately. Kidnapping, the crowd thinks. The woman has kidnapped the boy. She looks respectable but the boy is barefoot. He must have been playing around the house. She must have taken advantage of him, lured him away with some sweets or a poison. That's why he has vomited. They do not know her here, not her or the boy. One of the women pulls her hair. Another slaps her face. The boy goes berserk with grief. He tries to throw himself at the women who would be his avenging angels. They think he is seeking protection. One of them sweeps him up in her arms. He begins to wail in earnest, sure that he is going to be separated from his mother. Black Pants slips away through the crowd.

'How old was I?'

'I don't know. Maybe two or three.'

The women take her to the police station.

'Didn't you explain?'

'I was trying to tell them about the voices.'

'Why not tell them I was your son?'

'I didn't think of that.'

At the police station, Em gives the inspector-in-charge a number to call. An hour or so later, The Big Hoom is in the police station.

'He must have been in a great mood.'

'Oh don't. He was. But he couldn't say a word to them.'

I knew why he couldn't. Somewhere, there was a file. Somewhere, there was a file with a bus conductor in lotus pose, perhaps. Money had changed hands and the police had promised that the file had been wiped clean but no one could be sure. Suicide was a crime, the only one where you could be punished for failing. The Indian Penal Code lays it down clearly under Section 309: 'Whoever attempts to commit suicide and does any act towards the commission of such offence, shall be punished with simple imprisonment for term which may extend to one year (or with fine, or with both).'

So you could be miserable enough to kill yourself but the law will pay no heed to misery. It's an old law, a colonizer's law for the colonized, and it's not such a stupid law as it looks. How else to throw a troublemaker, fasting unto death, into jail? How else to deal with the likes of Gandhi?

But then, what of the Jain monks who simply stop eating and drinking? What of Vinobha Bhave, who decided it was time and went peaceably? The law could turn a blind eye if it wanted.

In Em's case, it had done that, helped by a little of The Big Hoom's hard-earned money.

But it might change its mind this time. We simply went home.

A few days later, we got a telephone. This in itself was a magnificent feat. A telephone line was not an easy thing to acquire. It required intervention at the ministerial level, even if you had a valid reason, such as a 'heart patient' in the house. Few people had phones and those who did often found themselves with a dead instrument. This gave rise to some dramatic protests such as the instrument being carried in a funeral procession through the streets.

'He made me swear to call him the next time the voices spoke to me,' Em said.

This fragile thing, the word of a woman who was mentally ill, was what kept the family going. We could not afford full-time nursing. And even when we could and did have a nurse, things still went very badly wrong. A nurse had been present when Em had slit her wrists, a nurse who had fallen asleep on the one afternoon when she should not have been sleeping.

So all we had was Em's word.

'You won't do anything silly?' The Big Hoom would ask her before he left in the morning.

'No,' she would say and her voice would sometimes be a sick moan. 'No.'

He would hug her and for a moment, her brow would clear, but soon he had to be gone and she would be shivering and hugging herself and asking for another Depsonil or death or a beedi. Even smoking was not a pleasure on her bad days. She would inhale deeply as if looking for something in the first fumes and when she did not find it, the despair would be back. The surcease was for a second only and after a couple of puffs, she would drop the beedi, literally drop it, sometimes burning her clothes, often letting it extinguish on the floor. The good thing about beedis is that they go out almost immediately.

Held by a single 'No' and by those beedis, she would wait for him to return. When he did, she would immediately ask for release.

'Kill me.'

'I might go to jail,' he would say patiently. 'Do you want that?'

'No,' she would say, but her voice would hold no real belief. She did not care one way or another. I remember the hurt I felt when he tried another tack once.

'I might go to jail,' he said, 'and who would look after the children?'

'I don't know,' she said and she didn't have to add, 'I don't care'. Both Susan and I knew it was the subtext. It was easy to forgive; we could see how much pain she was in. It was not easy to forgive; her pain sealed her off from us.

But how did The Big Hoom forgive? How did he hold on?

'All is Discovered. Let us Flee.'

When Em and The Big Hoom set forth on their new conjoined life, the Republic was relatively young and its coffers were empty. Salaries were low, prices were high and the middle class was expected to do its bit by saving as much as it could. Taxes were high and given the foreign exchange regulations and the exchange rate, no one thought of going abroad.

And yet, from all that I could gather, they had been happy. Improbably happy. Their world was clearly vulnerable, as if everyone was walking a tightrope over a smoking volcano. The ship of state could have foundered anytime, and repeatedly, plunging them into an abyss of debt. But none of that seems to reflect in their small black-and-white pictures of the time. Most of the pictures are pretty standard, taken at office parties, the occasional picnic and church weddings. Some, however, are odd: Em trying to smile in a silk sari; The Big Hoom at his desk in the office.

Who could have thought of taking that latter picture? It wasn't as if there were instamatic cameras in every purse or pocket. Film was rare and often had to be bought on the black market. You didn't just take a picture. You composed it with care. And that meant you took the kind of picture that everyone else was taking. This kind of picture, man at desk in office, isn't the kind I have seen in many other people's albums. Perhaps it has something to do with my father being the first generation of office workers in a family of peasants. It might well have been taken as a way of proving something to the village.

Those pictures tell a story. Imelda and Augustine were part of the dosa-thin middle class of the 1960s. They dressed like other young middle-class Indians of their background, they went to work in respectable, stable establishments and socialized in respectable, stable places. They also did their duties. They opened postal savings accounts and recurring deposits, put aside money for medical emergencies, bought units from the Unit Trust, had babies.

Susan was born two years into the marriage. I could not believe they had had the courage.

'Why would it take courage? I wasn't mad then,' said Em.

'Not that. Just the expense.'

'It wasn't expensive, because it wasn't a luxury. You got married. You had children. This was assumed. This was what people did. If you didn't do it, it was because you had a problem and people began to suggest adoption. We didn't buy a car because that would have been very expensive.'

Em had no recollections of being pregnant.

'I don't remember feeling much until I couldn't get into a rather nice pink skirt I had. Then I thought, "Oh, that's the baby," and wondered if I should give up working and all that. One cigarette later, everything was fine.'

'You were smoking when you were pregnant?'

'And did it harm you? Or Lao-Tsu? Not as far as I can see. You were a big fat lump and my poor vagina was never the same, though Il Santo never complained.'

'Em.'

'It's true. Natural birth was all the thing and the whole ward at St Elizabeth's was filled with women in pain. "Nurse, give me another Miltown," an Anglo-Indian lady would moan every ten minutes from the next bed.'

'They gave her sedatives?'

'Oh no, they didn't, the dirty bitches. They thought you should suffer. I remember a priest coming in on Sunday and reading out of the Genesis. It had to do with Adam and Eve and their apple. Apparently, we were supposed to suffer. Birth was supposed to be painful and we were suffering in expiation of Eve's sin. Adam got away, of course. Men do.'

The Book of Genesis is quite clear on the subject. The Lord God himself weighs in with 'I will greatly multiply thy sorrow and thy conception; in sorrow thou shalt bring forth children.' When anaesthesia was invented, the Church ranged itself against the use of painkillers in the maternity ward. That would be going against the curse of God Himself. It took Queen Victoria's insistence on a squirt of nitrous oxide, before doctors – and mothers too – decided that it wouldn't be a bad thing to lessen the worst pain known to humankind.

'My story sort of ends there,' Em said. 'What's to tell about the rest? You came along and I became a Mudd-dha.'

That word again. That venom. Maybe they should have thought about it, not just had a child because everyone did.

'I didn't think it was such a big deal. I don't know if LOS felt the same way about becoming a Dad. Not that he wasn't a complete seahorse. I don't think a man could have been happier when he had his first child. And then when the second one came along . . .'

Me.

'. . . he was over the moon. Then I slung my lasso at him and dropped him down to earth. But he took that in his stride as well. I told him, "Put me away." '

I remember one of the many days on which she had made the plea.

There was an account in the dim grey bank down the road, the cheque book locked up in the Godrej cupboard which sang and creaked whenever anyone tried to open it – 'Our built-in burglar alarm,' Em called it. The account was operated by Em and The Big Hoom, and it was money to be used 'in an emergency'. We knew without being told what 'emergency' meant: something happening to The Big Hoom. It was sacred money because, to Susan and me, at least, it carried the terror of being alone in the world. It was the worst possible nightmare we could conceive because we had no idea what we would do if we had to do it all on our own: monitor her pills, decide when she went to hospital, hold on to her life with a daily promise, pay her bills, take her raging or desperate calls, earn a living.

And one day, the truth came out.

From time to time, The Big Hoom would make Susan and me sit down and try to understand how the world of money worked. He would talk us through the notion of the stock market and the interim dividend, the public provident fund and the fixed deposit. He would make us fill out an application form for a bank loan or for the initial public offering of a company. It was his way of trying to prepare us for a world without him. The last step of this would be an explanation of the bank accounts: what was where and how it was to be used. He would explain about capital and running expenses and the need to forecast our expenses. He would show us how he did it, with a large heading called 'Imelda' under which he placed forty per cent of the annual income.

'Forty per cent?'

'It's gone above that some years,' he said briefly. I knew which years. The suicide years. 'But mostly, it comes in a little less and allows for some flexibility.'

And finally we would come to the bank down the road.

'This is to be kept in reserve,' he would say. 'For emergencies.'

At which point Em would say something like, 'Over my dead body, please.'

This time, she was silent.

Then, as if girding herself up, she said, 'There's nothing left in that account.'

There was a moment of silence.

'What?' His voice was ordinary, his everyday voice.

'I took it all out.'

'When?'

'I don't know.'

He got up and went into the bedroom. In ten minutes, he came out dressed. He left without saying a word.

'Oh shit,' said Em.

'What did you do?'

'I don't have to answer to you,' she said.

This was true, of course. It wasn't our money. But it was, in a way. In a terrible future way. It was difficult to point that out to her.

'I hate this whole money shit,' said Em. 'Do you remember that Lawrence poem? You studied it in college. Something about a pound.'

'The Madness of Money' by D. H. Lawrence. I knew it well. We knew all our poems well. We learnt them by heart and we learnt the summaries by heart. We did not learn anything about poetry, but we could tell a metaphor from a metonymy. And I could quote at random:

'I doubt if any man living hands out a pound note without a pang;/ and a real tremor, if he hands out a ten-pound note.'

'So,' said Em, as soon as I had finished, 'what if I was testing myself? What if I thought, I shall write a cheque without a pang?'

'Were you?'

'No. But I'm going to see my mother.'

'I don't think you should,' said Susan.

'I think I should. Suppose he kills me?' and here she gave a delicate stage shudder. We could see how worried she was, not because she really thought he would kill her, but because she had done something very wrong. Yet she was making it a performance, which was annoying.

'Don't be stupid,' said Susan. 'I'll make a cup of tea.'

'I love you forever,' said Em. 'But this is not the time for tea. It is time to write notes that say, "All is Discovered. Let us Flee."'

'Who to?' I asked.

'To Mae, who else?'

'You gave her the money?'

'I will not endure this interrogation from my own children,' she said. 'Oh where are my beedis?'

Susan pointed out that Em had them, as she always did, in the pocket of her housecoat. Em lit one and tried to hold on to being aggrieved but the pose cracked.

Finally, she said: 'Should I run or should I stay?'

'Where would you run to?' asked Susan logically.

'To my mother,' Em replied.

'Don't be childish. That's not even running.'

'What would Angela Brazil have you do?' I asked.

It was a stupid question but the Anglophile in my mother brightened.

'Well, I think I should Stay the Course,' she said. 'And I should Face up to the Consequences. Then maybe I should put a gun in my mouth and shoot myself before I am black-balled at the club. But I don't even have much luck at that.'

The wait wore us down, but in the end, she did not run. The Big Hoom came back and said nothing. Em tried to match his silence but could not. She kept breaking down and asking his forgiveness.

'There's nothing to forgive,' he said each time and his voice was normal and terrifying.

After a little while when the pressure got to her, she changed around and started saying that it was her money too because the account had been in her name.

'If you see it that way,' he said.

Time inched along. I remember trying to read and failing. Susan was working on a crossword. Only The Big Hoom seemed to be going about as if nothing had happened. When you live in a small house, your lives intersect all the time. There's no privacy, no way to conceal what is happening. Neither Susan nor I ever stormed off to our rooms and slammed the door and locked the world out, because neither of us had a room. Our lives were contained in a single bedroom and a single living room. There was a kitchen too and a toilet separated from the bathroom – which was an inordinate luxury – and four lives had to be managed within those walls. We had to live and love and deceive within earshot of each other.

'I can't tell you where the money went,' said Em defiantly.

'I can't remember asking,' he said.

'Don't be sarky,' she said.

'I'm sorry,' he said.

'No, I'm sorry,' she said. She even meant it but it broke the storm.

'You're sorry? You're *sorry*? Is that all you can say? You break the faith and you say you're sorry?'

'What faith?'

'The faith I have in you as a mother. The faith I have in you as a wife. The faith I have in you that you might have shifted some of your allegiance to this family.'

'I have. I have. Oh why didn't you listen to me and put me away when I told you to?'

It seemed like we were listening to an argument that was old and worn, being dragged out into the open. But I could not remember hearing this argument before. Could they have had it when we were asleep? I didn't think so. Both Susan and I were light sleepers, attuned to Em's emotional changes. If she started walking about too much, we woke up. When she spoke, we woke up. When she was lonely in the late night or in the early watches of the morning, all she had to do was start talking 'to herself' and one of us would be up sooner or later, crabby and irritable. 'Why did you get up?' she would ask disingenuously. 'You need your sleep.' 'Shut up,' Susan or I would say. 'Make tea.' And she would and we would begin to wake up and begin to talk. Sometimes, if we were very tired, she would send us back to bed and pretend to sleep herself.

During exam time, it was the unwritten rule that The Big Hoom would do the honours. Perhaps that was when they had discussed money?

Now The Big Hoom was looking at her in a way we had never seen. Not indulgently, not as a responsible brother looking at a younger sibling, not as the lover who seemed to ask for nothing in return, but as a trusting man injured in friendship, and surprised by the hurt.

'You have?' he asked quietly.

'In what way have I not?' demanded Em, though she sounded uncertain.

'If I had fallen down dead and you had needed some money, what would you have done?'

'I'd have asked Gunwantiben.'

There was a moment of silence. It was chilling.

'You would? You would go out and beg?'

'It wouldn't be begging. It would be a loan.'

'A loan? A loan like the ones your family has taken? It has a history of loans. And everyone plays along when they actually know that you people are begging.'

'Begging?'

'What do you think it is when you take a loan, then you take another loan, and you pay some of the first loan with the second? What do you think it is when someone gives you money and then writes it off? It's called begging.'

'Gunwantiben would not . . .'

'I am not talking about Gunwantiben. I am talking about you. I am talking about you turning your children into beggars. I am talking about how you cannot be trusted to keep even a single account inviolate.'

'I needed the money.'

'You needed the money?'

And then he suddenly looked across at the two of us transfixed by this discussion and seemed to decide that it was not worth it.

'I am sure you needed the money,' he said, without expression.

'Don't act like that.'

'I'm sorry,' he said. He was slowly packing it away.

'You're shutting me out.'

'Am I?' his voice was pleasant now. Almost. 'And since you cannot tell me why you needed the money, what are you doing?'

'I don't know. That's different. I think it's a matter of honour.'

'Is it? And does your code of honour allow you to steal from your children?'

'For the love of Mike,' Em snarled. 'It's not as if they're likely to starve.'

After that, The Big Hoom would not be drawn. Finally, Em decided that she had had enough. She walked out of the house and went to her mother.

We watched, almost without breathing, until he followed soon after.

They were back an hour later. They seemed to have resolved the money thing.

I had always been puzzled by how completely uninterested Imelda's parents seemed to have been in getting her married. But of course there had been a sound economic reason. She was the only earning member of the family.

Money had always been a problem, even when it was not supposed to be:

Finally had it out with them. What am I supposed to take with me? I mean, I know dowry is wrong and all that, but what happens to me if I go with empty hands? Surely, there is some money left over from ten-twelve years of working. But there isn't. Mae simply burst into tears and Daddy went to bed and turned his face to the wall. At five o'clock. Finally, as if by magic, as if summoned, Tia Madrinha turned up and said that Agostinho was a good man and had not asked so we should all say a decade of the rosary in thanks.

What power there is in a decade of the rosary! (Oddly, we had to say it to a sorrowful mystery because it is a Friday – although we were saying it in rejoicement, which should be the opposite of lamentation.) Daddy woke up. Mae agreed to let me make a cup of tea to cheer her up and Tia Madrinha took off her own gold chain and put it around my neck.

'You are my god-daughter,' she said sternly. 'I should not wear a gold chain if I have not given you one.'

But she looked bereaved almost as soon as she had done this and an imp of mischief made me want to take her gift seriously. But there had been enough tears and drama for several lifetimes so in the spirit of the thing, I took it off and put it back on her neck and said something about how the thought was gift enough. That settled that and I said I wanted to go to church and make my confession which was of course a way to simply rush off and be alone for a bit.

Took myself to Byculla. The area around the elephants is very soothing. I wish I were an elephant. I would be so composed.

But of course a walk in the maidan outside the zoological gardens in Byculla can only take you so far. After a while, she stopped walking. 'Almost fell into the arms of some young men,' she said.

'They might have enjoyed that,' I suggested.

'You think?' she said. 'They were kissing. Homos, I think.' She took the bus to Dadar.

'Jovial Cottage. What a terrible name. I couldn't bear it. I kept thinking of back-slapping drunken men and false smiles. I don't even know why they would bring Jupiter into it.'

'You're losing me.'

'Jovial? Jovial. Jove. Jove is Jupiter. Would you name your home for Jupiter? He seems to have been a thoroughly terrible fellow. Kept sleeping with his sisters and then cut off his father's balls and threw them into the sea. Can you imagine?'

Somewhat startled by the arrival of his fiancée in a state close to despair, Augustine rose to the occasion.

'He didn't even allow me to come in. Bad for my reputation, he told me. Instead, we went off to have tea. I don't remember where we went but I remember thinking that it was as bad for my reputation. After all, you didn't sit in an Irani restaurant with a man.'

'Not even a fiancé?'

'Not even. The rule was pretty clear. If you were a woman, you had better be with your father or your husband in an Irani.'

163

It was here that Augustine made one of those incidental remarks that would take root in his wife's head.

'I don't have a dowry,' she said baldly when they were served.

'I don't care,' he said.

'Your family will.'

'They won't.'

'How can you say that?'

'Because I'll tell them that you'll bring your dowry every month.'

This was true. At that point in their lives, Imelda – employed at the American Consulate – was earning more than Augustine. His pay was linked to the sales of heavy machinery and the industry was in a slump. It would recover soon enough – India's tryst with gigantism meant that someone somewhere always needed another large chunk of metal – but till it did, she was outperforming him.

He didn't know it but Imelda was equally reassured and horrified by what he had said. She worked because she had to. There was no question about that in her mind. The family relied on her salary. If she did not earn, they would not eat, not eat well at any rate. So she earned. But she had not considered what work meant after marriage. In her diary, she wrote:

He said it as if he thought I was going to work for the rest of my life. I suppose I will but it gives me the megrims, as someone in a G[eorgette] H[eyer] novel would say. Not the work, actually, I don't mind that. Not even those darned reports with their pages and pages of numbers and the carbon copies and all the rest of that. Not even those confidential reports. I will never forgive William Turtle Turner for that stupid remark, 'She does not keep her desk very clean.' As if I were a slattern and my desk a pigsty. (Is that a mixed metaphor?)

It's just the . . .

She seems to have cut herself off there. But the problem was not really about working. It was about what would happen to her salary. She had assumed that it would continue to go to her mother. Augustine had assumed that it would go into the common kitty of their marriage. The next entry in the diary says as much:

My salary is my dowry. And I can't see how there can be anything wrong with that – except that nothing should be anyone's dowry. No one thinks much if one asks the boy what his prospects are. If money is not important on the girl's side then money should not be important on the boy's side either, not in this day and age at least.

Asked Mae.

Came right out and asked her the question: How will you manage when I am married and living in his house?

She said, We will see. This means nothing. I wish I could get her to see that this means nothing but there was no getting anything else out of her. It was ever so. I must live with uncertainty and I don't think I can handle it.

Until the time she married, Imelda had suffered the deprivations of never having enough money. She also never had to worry about how to spend it. That was someone else's department. She earned it and handed it over, every last paisa of it, to her mother. Augustine had never been able to understand how Imelda could do that.

'But don't you want to keep some of it?'

'No,' said Imelda simply.

'No?'

'No.'

It was a simple, uninflected response.

'Aren't there things you want to buy?'

'Yes,' Imelda said. 'But most of the things I want to buy, I'd never get from my salary so there's no point thinking about them. I want a boat, for instance. I'm not going to get a boat on my salary.'

'So dates.'

'Yes. I can buy dates.'

'But only if you walk home.'

'I like walking home.'

'You sound like some kind of saint,' Augustine said, exasperated.

'Do saints want boats? Maybe St Christopher. And maybe St John would have wanted a date or two when he was eating locusts and wild honey.'

'You sound as if you've worked it all out.'

'I haven't,' she replied. 'I don't understand money.'

'Means? What's there to understand?'

'I don't know how to run a house. I don't know how to budget. I don't know whether one should buy five kilos of rice and one kilo of daal or one kilo of rice and five kilos of daal. I don't know what a good price for pomfret is. I don't know whether we pay the methrani too much or too little or what we tip her for Christmas. I know we don't tip for

Diwali, which is something, I suppose. I don't know if I get a good salary or not. See? There's lots you have to know to understand money.'

'And so you just ignore it?'

'I'm like Sherlock Holmes. I won't crowd my attic with that which does not concern me.'

'Even if it means refusing to grow up?'

'Is that what I seem like to you?'

'I think you can't be grown up if you don't take charge of your economic life.'

'Yes, that might be one way of looking at it,' Imelda conceded. 'But I think of my way as *The Way of Water*.'

Augustine shook his head. 'I should never have given you that Watts book.'

'This isn't about Zen,' said Imelda. 'I didn't even read that book. Honestly. I don't understand Zen. It seems if you don't answer properly, or you're rude, people get enlightened.'

'Why are we talking about Zen? We were talking about you.'

'Couldn't be. I wouldn't have been distracted from such a delightful topic.'

'We were talking about your problem with money.'

'No, we were talking about *your* problem with my money.'

'And you said you were like water.'

'I am like water. I flow past money.'

'The lady doth protest . . .'

'If you say that, I'll get up and leave in a pale pink huff,' said Imelda.

But Augustine was right. If this was how their conversation about money went – and this was how Em recalled it to me – then she was indeed protesting too much. Because there were times when her mother's inability to handle a budget could irk her:

Once again, I must do without. I don't understand why. We got you a dress in November, is all Mae will say. November will be my birthday until I die. Christmas will also fall in December until I die. (Unless there's a cataclysm in the Holy Roman Catholic Church or the Gregorian calendar or both. God forbid. Though they might make it easier and turn all the months into thirty-day months and declare a five-day holiday with no dates at the end of each year. I wish I knew mathematics. Then I would know if I would still be a Sagittarian. Or has that something to do with the stars and where the sun is? Must ask Angel Ears.)

But when I said I had spotted a really nice piece of silk which I thought would do well for an Xmas festivity thingy, I was told in no uncertain terms that I must do without. I feel like the March sisters: Christmas isn't Christmas without any new clothes.

What does she do with my money?

I feel mean asking. Like a man in a melodrama. I can't bring myself to ask. Angel Ears says I earn a handsome salary and that should keep us nicely. But he doesn't know that I have to darn my underwear in the most alarming places and wear the same shoes for months after I can feel the road beneath my feet. But I feel if I do ask, she might well say, 'I spend it on all of us. Why can't you earn some more?' How would I do that? None of the AmConGen girls seem to need more than one job and they spend like sailors on shore leave. In ASL, it was different. Liddy, poor duck, gave tuitions to some Marwari kids. English? Or English and History, I think. And there was Gertie who stitched her own clothes and wore them with such an air that you felt you should ask her to make you up something, even if you knew that she wasn't very good. I gave her that lovely floral cotton thing and she made it so deedy, I never had the heart to wear it, even after I took off a whole cartload of satin bows and ornamental buttons. I just told her I had got fat and I needed to slim down. I will get fat at this rate. And all for the want of a horseshoe nail.

Acting on his idea that she was protesting too much, Augustine handed Imelda his first pay after their marriage. Only, she had got her first salary too and had planned on handing it over to him.

I remember The Big Hoom telling us, 'She looked like I'd dropped a snake into her lap.'

'It was all too much money,' said Em. 'My only impulse was to go out and spend all of it.'

But she didn't. For years, she handed over everything she earned to her mother and then to her husband. When she started giving all her money to Augustine, she found she had to steal it back. And she did so, with his knowledge and unwilling consent, until she broke down and could no longer go to work.

'He made me resign,' she would say angrily. 'Or I might still have had my job to fall back on.'

'Stop talking rot,' Susan or I would say. For The Big Hoom said nothing. He knew what we realized much later: the Consulate had allowed her to resign when she started adding her own, and very alarming, comments to diplomatic reports. 'Personal interpolations', they called them. I loved that phrase and when I used it, aged eight or thereabouts, Em could still laugh though the joke was on her.

Even on the single salary that The Big Hoom brought home, we should have had a better life, materially, than we did. I think The Big Hoom, before he was The Big Hoom, had plans for all of us. Em's illness forced him to rewrite them. We ate well and we had as many books as we wanted. But nothing else was given. No servants. No refrigerator. A television, in any case, was a luxury for the middle classes.

From time to time, we would petition for a fridge, especially when we returned from the home of someone who had one. How effortlessly cold things were served. How easily a meal could be put together from this and that and these and those, all on separate levels, all in separate containers, all sealed away for the future.

'Why do we need a fridge?' The Big Hoom would ask rhetorically. 'We have the city's best market next to us. We eat our food fresh.'

'But what about keeping things in the fridge?' Susan said.

'Like pedas,' I said. 'Remember how your office sent us that huge box?'

'And do you remember how long it lasted?' he asked. Susan laughed ruefully. Em chuckled too.

'Gosh, I had a leaky bum for days after that.'

'Chhee,' I said and Susan said and even The Big Hoom made a sound of displeasure. But we knew that the phrase was now enshrined in Em's vocabulary. She would use it whenever diarrhoea surfaced in anyone's life.

So we had the market, we had fresh food, and for everything that was left over, there was Em.

'Except for doodhi,' she reminded me, the friendly spectre at my shoulder. 'And elaichi-flavoured Horlicks. I couldn't stand that. But if we're talking about food and eating, you must never forget the tale of the sweet fugya.'

Of course. It isn't easily forgotten. There was a time when Em hadn't slept for three days, except for short catnaps, during which she would drop half-smoked beedis on the floor. The flat swelled and trembled with the fever of her restless energy and unending chatter. Then one afternoon, halfway through lunch, it all caught up with her.

'I'm going to take a nap,' she said and we heaved a sigh of relief. She went off to sleep, and her body took its revenge. She slept for sixteen hours, straight, during which one of us would drip some water on her lips every four hours or so.

Then she woke up, much refreshed and ready to roister again. And began chewing.

'Hmm,' she said, 'this is a very sweet fugya'

Everyone stopped what they were doing. We had been eating fugyas – bread balls, slightly sweet, to be consumed with fiery hot sorpotel – at the meal from which Em had risen to take a nap.

'No wonder it's sweet,' said The Big Hoom. 'The saliva in your mouth has been working on it for sixteen hours.'

She had walked away from the table with a fugya in her mouth. Felled by the lack of sleep, she had succumbed with it still in her mouth. It was only some miracle that had prevented it from slipping down the wrong passage and killing her.

But then, she lived under some magic star as far as her body was concerned. She smoked for the greater part of her life and for most of it she suffered from a terrible hacking cough.

One day, things turned serious. She mentioned in passing, to Susan, 'my cauliflower'. Susan told me when I got home from college.

'You know, I didn't know what she was talking about. It could have been any part of her body but somehow, it made me stop. I said, "What cauliflower?" She said, "The one growing on my tongue." I said, "Show it to me," and she did.'

We both went back to peer into her mouth. Her tongue had a deep fissure on it, and in the middle of the fissure was a whitish growth, very like a cauliflower.

We freaked.

'Should we call him now?' I asked.

'I think not,' said Susan. 'It doesn't look like an emergency.'

I thought about it.

'Yeah, I don't think it's going anywhere right now.'

'You will not tell him,' said Em.

'Are you nuts?'

'I'll make you a deal. Let's wait until my birthday. If it's still there, you can tell him.'

Her birthday was two weeks away.

'What do you think is going to happen?'

'It's going to vanish.'

'You're mad or what?' I asked.

'*You're* mad or what?' Susan asked me.

But Em had an answer: 'I plead the fifth amendment.'

'The fifth amendment to the Indian Constitution concerns the relationship between the Centre and the states,' I said.

'Save me from this pedantic brute,' Em said.

Susan started in: 'Shut up. She has can –'

'Don't say it,' shouted Em. We couldn't tell whether this was common-or-garden superstition, or one more symptom: 'They' might hear.

'Okay, you have a cauliflower in the middle of your tongue . . .'

'Much nicer. I like cauliflower. I don't want a crab in the middle of my mouth.'

'Well, if you don't, you should stop smoking.'

'I am not going to stop anything.'

There was to be no discussion.

'May I see it again?' I asked.

'Certainly,' said Em and stuck her tongue out.

'Bejasus. That certainly looks like . . .'

'Don't say it.'

'Okay, but we're going to have to tell The Big Hoom.'

'You are not. I told you. It won't be there on my birthday. If it is, well, shoot me.'

'The point is not to have you die,' Susan pointed out.

Thinking about it now, I cannot believe that we did not rush her to an oncologist right there. But we didn't. Because we were used to the idea of Em being in a medical emergency of some kind or the other.

And on her birthday, we checked her tongue, Susan and I. No cauliflower.

'What happened?' I asked.

'I don't know,' she said. 'But I told Our Lady, I am not going like this. So she took it away.'

I didn't know what to make of this miracle.

'What happened?' Susan asked. Her tone was different. She wasn't taking any of that.

'It detached itself and I swallowed it,' said Em.

173

'Ick,' said Susan but she seemed satisfied with that.

'Can we tell him now?'

'Tell him about what?'

'Your cauliflower.'

'What cauliflower?' she said, her eyes wide open. But The Big Hoom entered the room carrying a tray of bacon and eggs and toast, her favourite breakfast. He heard too.

'What cauliflower?' he repeated. He had a way of scenting the important. I told him. He looked at both of us. Then he looked at her. All of us wilted a bit. We ate our breakfast in silence. Finally, Em broke the silence.

'It's gone,' she said.

He said nothing.

'She made us promise,' I said.

He said nothing. When breakfast was over, he made a phone call. Em was to go with him to the doctor. When it was all fixed, he said to both of us: 'Sometimes, I wonder whether education really matters.'

Then he left for work.

Em tried to cheer us up.

'Nothing's wrong with me.'

'This isn't about you,' said Susan.

'We should have told him,' I said.

'No, we should have taken her to a doctor ourselves.'

'You and whose army?' asked Em, truculent. It was one of her favourite phrases. The marines posted at the AmCon-Gen had used it a lot.

But the miracle continued. She was examined thoroughly, pinched and prodded, scanned and sounded and even had 'a finger put up my bum after due warning from a sweet Malayali girl'. But nothing was found.

'Lungs like bags of phlegm. Voice like a pross on the prowl. Cough like a lion in the Serengeti. But no crabs in the body, no crabs in the crotch. I beat the odds. How's that? I would like to donate my body to science, you bounders, so that they can find out what exactly made me immune. Break out the bids, folks,' she chortled.

'So what was the cauliflower?'

'You silly berks can't tell a ruddy miracle when you see one?"

'No.'

'Oh ye of little faith. How shall ye be ducks in the gardens of paradise were I not there to wish it for ye?'

'I don't recognize that from any version of the Bible,' I said.

'It's my version,' said Em, bubbling. 'I shall be swanning about in the promised land and you two will get a good ducking.'

'Stop it,' I snarled.

'Em,' said Sue.

'I told Our Lady . . .' she trailed off. 'Okay, I said to her: take five years from my score but let me go eating and drinking and smoking. You gave me this stuff . . .' she tapped her forehead, 'and I took it with good grace.'

'Good grace?'

'You have to live through what I've lived. You'd think it good grace too. So I said, take five years. Obviously, someone was listening. Lady in blue, I love you. That's why I told you, I can't take too much more male will in my life. No thy-will-be-done for me. I surrender nothing. I surrender nothing. I'll take my chances with a woman's kindness.'

'Electro-Convulsive Throppy'

On a college trip to the Thane Mental Hospital, I had seen what I thought was the worst of India's mental health care system. Thirty or so third-year students with an interest in psychology, we were shepherded there by Arpana Shetty, a junior lecturer, so junior that she had just finished her masters and was seen as a suitable object for lechery. We were introduced to Sunil, a drug addict who was in recovery – or so the hospital claimed. He was obviously a young man from the middle class or above. He spoke English well and without self-consciousness, as to the manor born.

'You can get anything here,' Sunil said peaceably. 'It's all part of the way India works.'

'I don't understand,' said Arpana.

'Free your mind, Ms Shetty,' said Sunil. 'This is a poor country with good topsoil. A poor country pays its people poorly. They can be bought and sold easily enough.'

'Sunil . . .' said a voice behind us. It was someone who looked like a bureaucrat. Arpana Shetty presented her credentials. As the bureaucrat examined them and introduced himself, Sunil continued to address us, his gaze abstracted, his manner gentle.

'I am only saying that if you give a poor man a poor man's

pay and good topsoil, he will sow some seeds and grow some greens and sell them to the first bidder,' said Sunil.

'Sunil, what lies are these?' asked Mr Shinde, the psychiatric social worker of the hospital, for that was who the bureaucrat was. Sunil smiled at him gently.

'I am only saying these things in a hypodermic manner, you understand,' he said.

'Hypothetical, you mean?' asked Marina, a girl who would have been beautiful if she had had a chin.

'Do I?' Sunil asked. 'I must go now and cut myself some envelopes to prove to the world that I am a socially useful and productive person.'

Then he turned and ambled off, his minders gently urging him on when he slowed down, or redirecting him when he tried to wander away.

'He got arrested,' Shinde explained. 'The court said jail or here. Here means no criminal record so his parents put him here. He will go home in two months.'

A crocodile of patients went past. They all looked alike in dirty grey white clothes and near-shaved heads. They looked dehumanized, as if their identities had been stolen. They looked like something from a Holocaust film.

'Where are they going?' Arpana asked Shinde.

'Electro-Convulsive Throppy,' said Shinde. 'ECT. Shock treatment.'

We had learnt about it in abnormal psychology. James Coleman, who had written our text book, was sure that this treatment had outlived its utility and spoke with heavy irony of how the Russians still reported great results from its use in state mental hospitals. He seemed to be suggesting that the socialists would do anything to maintain their quotas.

'Can the students watch?' Arpana asked.

Shinde nodded as if it were a matter of indifference to him. He was casual, as if granting her the right to use the toilet in his house. It occurred to me then that the mad in India are not the mentally ill, they are, simply, mad. They have no other identity. Here, everyone was mad. They had lost their hair so that the institution could keep them free of lice. They had lost their clothes because their families had abandoned them, and they had lost their lives because they had lost their families. They were now free, in a bizarre sort of way. They were also alone except for the shoulder in front and the touch of the fingers of the person following behind.

No wonder Shinde did not ask their permission. No one asked their permission. They did not need to be asked. I thought it would be disconcerting meeting their eyes because I wouldn't know what was going to look out or what I was going to be looking into. But in the line I found nothing much. An old woman who was looking at everyone with venomous eyes. A man who seemed to be stripping the women. And then a young man who smiled at me, a smile of such awesome sweetness that I felt I had found the key.

The key was me.

Add me and the mentally ill could be saved. The young man was healed. He had reached out. But then I noticed that the smile came and went like something mechanical. He did not even seem to notice who he was smiling at.

The line dissolved at the door of the dispensary. One of the ward boys used his body as a battering ram and got everyone into line again. The first mad person, a man of indeterminate age, lay down on a table and a cup was placed by his side. The next two patients strapped him down while he struggled weakly, almost as if by habit. They stepped back. The electricity was turned on. The patient's body arched. Then he relaxed. His head was turned over and saliva came bubbling, frothing out of his mouth. Then the switch was thrown again and he went into a spasm. Then the next two patients undid the straps, rolled him off and helped him to stumble groggily to the side of the room where he slumped, as if his bones had melted, into a heap on the floor. His legs were splayed, his head drooped on his chest and some last drops of saliva ran down his chest.

It was like watching some ancient medicine man at work. Even in the late 1980s, it was old juju.

'It has a remarkable success rate,' said Arpana defensively. Shinde seemed to have vanished.

'What is success?' Ravi asked. He was a sharp-faced and silky-haired boy from my university, with a quicksilver mind. It glittered but it had no staying power. You could tell he would go on to become a huge success in advertising.

I could have told them both what success meant, what ECT did, but I held my peace.

Later, Arpana told us that she knew of a doctor who administered ECT to a fourteen-year-old girl who had started wetting her bed and a twenty-four-year-old who had memory lapses.

'Did it cure them?' Ravi asked.

'It helped them.'

'And how exactly?'

'It helped them to be normal,' said Arpana with the ease of someone who had never really been interested in words.

'So the end of psychiatric medicine is to iron out all differences and produce identical paper dolls?'

'I didn't say that.'

'Well, the word normal comes from "norm" and the norm . . .'

'. . . allows for deviation,' said Arpana triumphantly.

'And the limits for that are set by the word normal?' Ravi asked.

'Yes.'

'Who sets the limits?'

For a moment, I could clearly see how this would shape up. Ravi was going to beat the shit out of Arpana with his mind. He was going to demonstrate his intellectual superiority. He was going to show us his debating skills. The rest of the debate wound its way past R. D. Laing, definitions of normalcy, the state of middle-class morality, the issue of Marxist analysis, and other bits and pieces of our sophomore reading.

But a question stayed with me. What is a cure when you're dealing with the human mind? What is normal? I saw Em at that moment, the time she went into the Staywell Clinic: a raving maniac, her face flushed, a blob of frothy spit caught between her lips, her hair wild, her voice cracked and harsh, her eyes flickering incessantly, as she assessed the flood of information that was her world for new threats to all of us . . .

No, that's not quite how it was.

Em didn't go into the Staywell Clinic. We sent her there. Susan and I.

In the fading light of Li_2CO_3, Em decided that there was a conspiracy aimed at her. Soon, she was sure that it was aimed at the entire family. The Brihanmumbai Mahanagarpalika, the municipal corporation of the city, had decided to dig up the roads outside our house. The trenches looked like graves to Em and she became convinced that the architects of the conspiracy were winning. There was nothing left to do but appease them. They demanded offerings, and so late one night she began to throw things into the trenches. A clock hit a sleeping worker, some of our household goods were flung back at us, with shrill abuse, and the neighbourhood was roused. 'They', who would bury us in unmarked graves under Mahim's roads, had demanded our alarm clock, several handkerchiefs, The Big Hoom's watch, spoons, katoris, glass toffees, ashtrays and some of my college books.

At three o'clock in the morning, it seemed like a horrible calamity. When one was surrounded by neighbours who could not decide whether to be angry at having their sleep disturbed or vastly intrigued by the goings-on, when one had just had a couple of years of comparative peace, this seemed to be the last straw for me. I began to scream and wail and carry on in the manner of the people I despised most. I screamed that I was leaving the house. I said I could not live with someone like that. I said I wanted to kill myself. I said I could not bear my life. Perhaps if The Big Hoom had been in town, it might have been different. But he wasn't. He had been offered the chance of a lifetime; an opportunity to earn some money in Brazil, on deputation for the Indian government.

'It's only because I speak Portuguese,' he had said when he told us he would be away.

I felt my heart sink. I was to be the man of the house?

'Granny will come and stay here,' he continued, and I began to bristle. What did we need Granny for?

Granny had agreed with me, but she came. She had nothing

much to do for several days. Em and she sat around and chatted desultorily. Em sang hymns and made some 'personal interpolations' at which Granny clucked in perfunctory and half-hearted disapproval. Tea was consumed in large quantities and mealtimes were full of unexpected excitement since Granny cooked happily for four.

But on the day before the storm, Granny had been tempted to go off to the novena at St Michael's church. She was going to say it nine times in a single day for her daughter's health. When she came home the following morning, she began to wail and blame herself. We were all distraught. I thought I might cry so I started to shout again. Susan told me to shut up. Em said irritably, 'Oh stop it. I'll go to hospital.'

Then she went off to bed, exhausted.

We agreed, Susan and I, that this was a cry for help. Was it? Or was it us, hoping for some peace and quiet? At any rate, Em felt at home in Ward 33 of Sir J. J. Hospital. It was as much a government hospital ward as any. The schizophrenics and the anorexics and the depressives were locked in with the alcoholics and the drug addicts. None of this seemed to matter to Em. She always slipped into the ecosystem without much effort. Divorced from decision-making, she soon became the star patient. She would change from the raving ranting harridan who smoked and shrieked and threw things out of the house into Nursie's Little Helper. She would feed the recalcitrant and collect the pills that they spat out. She would urge gentleness on the ward boys and chat in broken Hindi to everyone. Perhaps this was just strategy, a way to avoid ECT, but it worked. She went to Ward 33 willingly, even when she was depressed and wanted to die. Perhaps the rhythm of hospital life soothed her, suited her. Here, no decisions were to be made and no one expected you to be anything other than a survivor, lying on a somewhat grubby bed, waiting for the tide to rise again. It might even have been the home she kept asking for. 'Put me in a home,' she would moan. There was no answer to this because there were no homes for the mentally ill, not unless you wanted to take your chances with the mental hospitals and ECT.

However, this time the ward was full. There was not a mattress on the floor to be had although one more could always be squeezed in. All you had to do was claim that your patient was suicidal and the hospital would be obliged to take her in. But since Em was in full form – already trying to bum beedis off ward boys and greeting ward sisters as if they were old friends, patting old women on the head and telling them that everything would be all right if they had 'bharwasa' in God – it was not an easy sell. This was what made everything about her illness so difficult to understand. If she had had a paranoid attack last night, where was it now? If she had been worried about her family being buried in the trenches of road repairs, why was she hugging a shy Malayali nurse and telling her that she was not to worry about being short because she had 'more inches to choose from'? Had she made some sort of pact? Had she worked it out in her head that if she went to hospital, we would all be safe? Or had the paranoia passed?

The answer was: any or all of the above.

What was not the answer was the one that always came to my overheated mind when something had happened that upset me: she was faking it. She was indulging herself. She was taking us all for a ride.

This was the lazy way. It was also a way of getting cheap

relief. For a few moments, everything was located squarely within the range of ordinary human emotions and motives. Em was not mad. She was simply another malingerer. Like any other malingerer, she wanted to evade her ordinary responsibilities. Like any other malingerer, she wanted to be served hand and foot. We had all been taken for a ride. We were fools.

I don't remember thinking this when she was depressed, for there was no way she could have been faking her depression.

But now, the terror and embarrassment of the night's chaos still fresh in my mind, I told myself, Yes, she's faking it, no way she's not faking it. This spared me the phenomenal expense of empathy. Unfortunately, it was not very convincing and did not last long. I could not convince myself that Em really wanted to laze around. She was always willing to make tea, to clean up in a desultory fashion if you insisted on cleanliness, to type out a play script so that it could be photocopied. She would help out with anything you wanted. And what could be the advantage that accrued to her in faking an attack of paranoia? While she did think of Ward 33 as a kind of second home, it was still second best.

'Full up?' she asked Matron Galgalikar in mock outrage. 'You're telling *me* you're full up? And me one of your best patients?'

'Arre, we would take you like that . . .' and here Matron Galgalikar snapped two plump fingers under Em's nose, '. . . but where will I put you? On my hip?'

'Nice hip,' said Em and allowed herself to be led back to the car and taken to the Staywell Clinic in Khar. On the way there, the rage returned. She lashed out at the cab driver.

She tried to pull off her clothes as payment. She began to sing raucously and then to beat herself. It was only when Susan burst into tears that she eased off a little.

The Staywell Clinic was run by Dr Alberto D'Souza, one of the city's senior-most psychiatrists. Had Alfred Hitchcock been born Indian, he would have looked like Dr Alberto. He was short, he was round, he was bald, he was lugubrious, his jowls sagged and his face was puffy to the point that it seemed as if the fat were restricting his freedom of expression. And he wore three-piece suits in defiance of Mumbai's subtropical weather. It was never a problem getting a bed at the Staywell Clinic. It had a high turnover because it was expensive.

A week later, she was returned to us as from the dry-cleaners'. We recognized her because she looked as she did in the intermediate stages – a crisp middle-aged Roman Catholic lady in a crisp, floral-printed cotton dress, leaning slightly on her husband's arm, for The Big Hoom had returned to take charge.

But we knew that something was wrong. We smelt it in the aura she exuded. We felt it in the way her eyes met ours. There was nothing in her eyes, none of the collusive appeal to family that she normally made. Something in her brain told us we were friends so she treated us like friends, but there was nothing behind it. And then we discovered that love was about memory and something had disrupted her store of our collective memories.

'Why have they tied up your hair?' Susan asked and reached forward to pull the band off Em's grey-black hair. Through the open window of the car, the hot breeze began to play with Em's hair. Em shook her head, shaking out her hair, a familiar gesture from a changeling.

Susan froze.

I followed the direction of her gaze. On the side of Em's forehead, a high forehead that remained unlined to the day she died, was a mark, a red angry mark, a burn mark, the place where the electricity had surged into her head.

We both looked out of our windows. Susan was crying, silently; I wanted to but couldn't find a way. The Big Hoom began to talk to Em, in a quiet rumble, like distant thunder.

When we were home, Susan made tea and we drank it in our usual positions: Em and Susan sitting at the table, The Big Hoom leaning on the kitchen counter and me on the floor. I can still see the scene in my head because it was one of the few times we were drinking tea at an appropriate moment in the day. Em sat like any of a million perfectly correct Roman Catholic women, her knees pressed together, her elbows off the table, her head inclining courteously to the person speaking. She was a caricature of herself. She drank her tea in polite sips. She accepted a refill with a 'Thank you' that pinged off two ugly notes. When she had finished, she put down her cup and sat, looking at the wall.

The silence began to suffocate us all. We were not used to it, nor were we used to breaking it. Susan took a spoonful of chivda and crunched her way through it.

'Nice chivda,' she said.

'Where is it from?' Em asked.

'Brijwasi,' said Susan, the slight surprise in her tone indicating that there were no choices in such matters.

'Is that close by?' Em asked and she might well have lobbed a hand grenade into the kitchen. Brijwasi was a local institution. Every child knew it because it had a range of delights from the dry fruits that only a few rich parents could afford to buy and hoard, to a street-facing counter of glass bottles that rose in steps – with the cheapest sweets at the bottom. Every child in the range of ten buildings from Brijwasi could tell you the order of the bottles. I could. Even now I have only to close my eyes and pretend that I have seventy-five paise with which to destroy my teeth . . .

Em could too.

She was the only adult I knew who loved sweets with the same animal passion as children. I watched with amazement as other mothers spooned their own desserts into the plates of their children. Neither Susan nor I could even think of asking Em to share her sweets. Her footsteps, and ours, always slowed as we passed Brijwasi and she gazed at the trays of mithai with as much longing as we did.

And now she had forgotten, and the world was lying askew around us. It was still functional. We could hear the buses and smell Gunwantiben in the next flat roasting ajwain for some fell culinary purpose. But to us the world was on its side as we sipped our tea.

Finally, The Big Hoom spoke.

'It's a sweet shop,' he said.

It was, after all, the answer to Em's question.

'This is not sweet,' said Em, pointing at the chivda.

Susan giggled. So did I. I cannot remember if we were even vaguely amused. I do remember that we were terrified.

'Don't you chaps have to hit the books?' The Big Hoom asked, and we left the kitchen in a rush. I buried myself in matrices; Susan began to read Adorno. It was what we did.

I grew up being told that my mother had a nervous problem. Later, I was told it was a nervous breakdown. Then we had a diagnosis, for a brief while, when she was said to be schizophrenic and was treated as one. And finally, everyone settled down to calling her manic depressive. Through it all, she had only one word for herself: mad.

Mad is an everyday, ordinary word. It is compact. It fits into songs. As the old Hindi film song has it, *M-A-D, mad mane paagal*. It can become a phrase – 'Maddaw-what?' which began life as 'Are you mad or what?'. It can be everything you choose it to be: a mad whirl, a mad idea, a mad March day, a mad heiress, a mad mad mad mad world, a mad passion, a mad hatter, a mad dog. But it is different when you have a mad mother. Then the word wakes up from time to time and blinks at you, eyes of fire. But only sometimes, for we used the word casually ourselves, children of a mad mother. There is no automatic gift that arises out of such a circumstance. If sensitivity or gentleness came with such a genetic load, there would be no old people in mental homes.

On that visit to the mental hospital in Thane, the city south of mine, I had felt bits of my heart go brittle and crumble as an old Anglo-Indian lady recited her address in a papery voice and said, 'Tell them to come, son. These people will not tell them. I am well now. See.' She showed me her case paper. 'Fit for discharge' was written on it.

I thought she had written it herself or faked it but when I checked with the warden, I was told that it was official. She was fit for discharge.

'So why don't you send her home?' I asked. 'I can take her.'
'What home?' the warden asked.
'Surely you have her address somewhere.'
'On the case paper. First look, no?'
I looked. To my shame, it was there.

'Home is not address,' said the warden. 'Home is family.'

'So where's her family?'

'Gone.'

'Gone?' I was startled but not much. In India, family might well be wiped out. 'No one left?'

'Arrey, they're all alive. They just left. Full family left. We paid for her to go back, in a taxi. But another family was living at that address and they had gone. No address. One of the neighbours said that they left like thieves in the night.'

'Maybe they were in debt?'

'Maybe.' But the warden did not sound convinced. 'Or maybe they wanted to make sure that she would not come back and be a bojh. This is a hospital but it is also used as a dumping ground, a human dumping ground.'

All the way back, I had felt sick and sad. And I was afraid.

Fight your genes, he had said. One of the defences I had devised against the possibility of madness was that I would explain every feeling I had to myself, track everything down to its source. After I returned from Thane, I worked it out on a piece of paper:

1. I might end up there. I feel sad at the thought.
2. That woman has ended up there. Ditto.
3. Em might end up there. This might be an escape route if anything happens to The Big Hoom. I feel sick that I should even have thought of this when I can feel sad at the thought of myself being there.
4. Susan. What if something happens to Susan? I look at her and she seems fine. But what if she isn't? Em probably looked fine to her parents. If something happens to Susan, can I do all this again?

My defences were flimsy. The enemy might already be inside my head and if that were the case, everything else was a straw in the whirlwind. Somewhere, with every meal I ate and every breath I took, I was nurturing the enemy. I thought of clamping down on the errant thought and recognized this as an errant thought born out of despair. I thought of counselling and all the faces of the counsellors I knew floated in front of me. They seemed kindly and distant. They were from that other place, the far side, the normal side. I could not afford therapy, and in any case, I had only the faintest notion of what it could do. It was depressing. There seemed to be nothing I could do: no preventive medicine, no mental health vitamins, no mind exercises in the cool of the morning.

The day I turned twenty-one, I stayed back late at the newspaper office where I worked, waiting for people to leave so I could make a private phone call. I called Dr Michael, one of Em's psychiatrists, the one she trusted most. On her first meeting with him, she had asked him in her forthright way: 'No more shocks?'

'Shocks?' he asked. 'Who gives shocks these days?'

'My children,' said Em.

'Mine too,' he said.

Em laughed.

Then she saw my face and covered her mouth in mock horror at what she had said.

'Oh dear,' she said to Dr Michael. 'I think someone is upset.'

'Who?' Dr Michael asked. 'He?'

'Yes,' said Em. 'But they did not mean it, the poor dears. They never do. They kill you with love and they don't mean that either. Every day shocks. Every day for ten days. So little of me was left when I came home. But what could they do, poor dears?'

Each time she used 'poor dears', she gave it a different spin, none of them pleasant. I tried to cast back to that horrible time for the explanations I had offered myself, that Susan and I had offered ourselves, and found that I could not. What she had done to us paled in front of what we had done to her.

'How are you now?' Dr Michael asked.

'How do you find me?' She cocked an eyebrow at him, armed in the full flush of mania, ready for battle, ready for friendship, ready for anything, terrified somewhere underneath the bravado that it might come to *that*. (We never found out what *that* was, but we knew that it was pretty high in the pantheon of her unspoken terrors.) Did Dr Michael see all this? Or did he see another Roman Catholic mad woman of a certain age in a flowery cotton frock and dirty toenails? What *did* he see? I wanted to protect her from his eyes and from the eyes of everyone else. I had failed and that made me angry with her and with myself. I could not explain this to the doctor; I wasn't even supposed to.

'I don't know you well so I can't tell. How much of you has come back?' he asked Em.

'How much do you think has come back?'

'I think you're one hundred per cent now.'

'I am one hundred per cent, doc.'

'So what's all this about, this "so little was left"?'

'Oh, he's a smart one,' said Em. 'But doc, we need to get this clear. Whose side are you on?'

'Yours.'

'I bet you say that to all your patients.'

'I do,' he said.

'Really? I thought you would have only said it to your wife.'

He laughed and then looked at her. It seemed as if he were taking stock of her again. Perhaps he did see something behind the woman in the cotton frock. But wasn't that his job? Or was it? A diagnosis helps cure. But it also pigeonholes the patient. She's manic depressive; he's schizophrenic. Into your box.

'I only say it to those who ask.'

'Then they should all ask.'

'Maybe if they didn't have problems, they would ask.'

'Because there's no point if you're not on my side.'

'I'm on your side.'

'Glad to hear that, Mike. Put it there, pal.'

She stretched out a hand, he shook it and Em settled into a trusting relationship with a psychiatrist. In doing so, she was exercising her right to hurt us. Dr Michael, on his part, never sent her to hospital except on one occasion and even then, she came back with the skin on her face intact. No shocks. It helped that as a Roman Catholic, he understood what she was talking about when she tried to explain how she had given up going to confession out of boredom.

'I told him about the twenty-six,' she said to me once. 'He said, "That's all old-fashioned now."'

Most of the time, the myth about the twenty-six transplanted foetuses worked. But that it was a story she told often revealed something else, I thought: the guilt she felt over using contraception and the guilt she felt about those strange leaps down the stairs, six times six, each of twenty-six times. This guilt had accompanied her for years and it was faintly galling that she seemed to be relieved of it just because Dr Michael had said that it was old-fashioned. I had been telling her pretty much the same thing. Susan had explained the patriarchy's claim on the body of women and how men always wanted to control the way women reproduced. The Big Hoom had said that it was nobody's business but hers and his. She had agreed with all of us. She nodded and smiled but we knew she was just being polite. Underneath, nothing changed. Then Dr Michael sorted that one out. Just by saying it was old-fashioned.

I was old enough to know that my resentment of this bond was shading into jealousy. I had always been the person she had trusted. She would only take her tablets from me. On the rare occasions that I was not around, she would take them, on instruction, from Susan. Now Michael was the new mantra. Susan called him the archangel.

'Dr Michael says . . .' became one of Em's favourite opening lines. It was also the most efficient way to close an argument with her. So although I hated him in a mild, milky way, I also respected something about him. He seemed, like The Big Hoom, to be made of some solid substance that could not be compromised. It might have been masculinity of the full-fledged, hair-in-the-ears, built-for-endurance, thick-around-the-middle sort.

That was why I called his clinic and made an appointment.

'When do you want to bring her?' he asked.

'This isn't about her,' I said. 'I want to meet you.'

I had read about pregnant pauses and I had always wondered if I could recognize one. I did.

'Is it urgent?' he asked after a while.

I assured him that it wasn't.

We met a week later in a generic room in a generic poly-clinic. Doctors played musical chairs with these rooms all over the space-starved city.

He looked at me quizzically.

'What's your problem, then?'

I didn't know how to say it so I said it straight.

'I want to know. Will I go mad?'

He considered me for a moment. He said nothing.

'Okay,' I said. 'I know you don't have a crystal ball. I'm asking what the chances are.'

'You can only watch and wait,' Dr Michael said. 'There's definitely a genetic component to bipolar disorders but no one can tell you whether you're going to get it or not.'

'Not a dominant/recessive thing, then?'

'No. Right now we talk about triggers, stress, lack of love, failure at work, that kind of thing. But I've seen people take some awful knocks and nothing happens. There's one thing though . . .'

I urged him on with my eyes and chin.

'If you get past your thirties, you're generally safe. If it hasn't happened by then, it won't happen at all. Or at least it becomes statistically improbable that it will.'

'Statistically improbable' was not enough. I wanted real assurance, or a diagnosis. When you're a child, cast the runes. When you're an adult, ask an expert. I had. The expert had no answer.

Wait. Watch.

12.

'Who wants a hot flush?'

Dr Michael came into our lives shortly after the Staywell Clinic (to which Em never returned), and soon we were depending on him more than we had on any other psychiatrist. He took to Em, or maybe he was like that with all his patients. 'Only a phone call away,' he told us, and he was. Em's dosages could now be fine-tuned almost from day to day, instead of from week to week.

Did it help?

It helped us to know that we were doing everything in our power. But it seemed as if all psychiatric medicine was aimed only at the symptoms. Mute the paranoia. Calm the rage. Raise the endorphins. Underneath, the mysteries continued, unchanged. Underneath, somewhere in the chemistry of her brain, there was something that could not be reached. I was always aware of this. I could not answer the question 'How's mum?' so I learnt a complicit smile. It worked because it drew the questioner into the penumbra of brave suffering that I manufactured for the world.

Physically, she seemed fine. We had almost never worried about her body. 'I'm as strong as a mule and twice as ornery,' she would often say when someone asked how she was. Her preferred diet was bhajiyas and sweet fizzy drinks for what 'they do to my tongue'. But even those paled when the beedis ran out. There were only two moments of fright. The time when the cauliflower appeared in the middle of her tongue. And then three years later, when she seemed to have a growth in her uterus.

After she turned fifty, Em suddenly began to look a lot fatter than she had ever been. We all put it down to something in her metabolism, something to do with the amount of sugar she could consume when she was high, six spoons in a single cup of tea, a handful just for fun if she were passing the sugar tin, any amount of chocolate or jalebis or sweets from Brijwasi. In times of shortage, this could be a problem since we would be forced to hide the sugar, but most of the time it was a matter of casual teasing and no one seemed to be bothered, least of all Em herself.

But one day, she went off on one of her missions of mercy, to see Sarah-Mae, the nurse. We were related to her in some distant complicated way that everyone in the family understood as a responsibility. Sarah-Mae had lost everything when her younger boyfriend Christopher had disappeared into Canada on what he called a 'recce mission'. Em would go see her twice a year at Saint Joseph's Home for the Aged in Bandra, when she could, to 'make her feel a little less lonely, the silly hag'.

This time, when she returned, she was looking all hot and bothered.

'I have to go to the hospital,' she said to me and Susan.

Both of us were startled.

'What happened? You going to do it again?'

'No, no. I'm superfine. No, no, actually, I'm not. Or maybe I'm not. But Sarah-Mae says it's a Growth.'

Sarah-Mae had few charms but she was a skilled nurse, when she wasn't drunk. She was born one of triplets, who had been lifted out from their mother, two of them conjoined at the head. It was also said that she had a black tongue, which meant that if she predicted something terrible it would come true. Of all the triplets, Sarah-Mae had had the worst time. Early on, she had sacrificed her left ear to Olivia-Mae because they were the two joined at the head – by the ear, and only one of them could have it. So Sarah-Mae's word was to be taken seriously.

Em was taken to a gynaecologist who suggested various tests and then an operation.

'At the J. J. Hospital,' said Em.

The Big Hoom suggested a drive that evening. He drove around the city with Em, late at night, when they had something to talk about or when everyone needed a break from her.

They came back hours later to find both of us awake.

'Let's have a cuppa,' said Em.

'What's happening?'

'She's going to J. J.,' said The Big Hoom.

Em began to boil some tea.

'When?' Sue asked.

'Tomorrow,' said Em and then she began to sing. 'It's now or never, come hold me tight . . .'

The Big Hoom went up and hugged her. We drank our tea quietly.

'If I die under the knife,' said Em suddenly, 'give whatever you can to whoever you can.'

'What does that mean?'

'Meaning, me bits and bobs. I don't want to be worm fodder. My bits would like a second chance. Someone looking out through my eyes. Someone loving with my heart. Someone having a good lash out with my liver.'

'Okay,' said The Big Hoom.

The next morning, they were gone and Granny was frying bacon and eggs when we got up.

'Come,' said Granny.

We sat down.

'They are thissing,' she said, 'we can only thissing.'

We enjoyed praying with Granny. She prayed in a mellifluous mess of syllables. The first half of the Ave Maria was reduced from 'Hail Mary, full of grace, the Lord is with thee, blessed art thou and blessed is the fruit of thy womb, Jesus' to 'Hail Meh fluh grace loswiddhee blessdaathou blessdfroo thaiwoom Jee-zus . . .' It was difficult not to giggle. If she noticed, it did not seem to bother her. She slurred on, simply slowing the words down. Perhaps they did not make sense to her, which wouldn't have been unusual.

That morning, however, we weren't giggling, or thinking about the meaning. We were simply praying. For our Em. We were not praying for her mind. We had not given up doing that, but we were losing hope that prayer could be part of the solution. We were praying for her body and it occurred to me that we had never had occasion to, before this. ('Strong as a horse,' Susan said when I pointed this out and for a week or so we called her The Horse.)

I tried to look now at the words we were saying and I could not see how they matched our needs. We seemed to be as anachronistic as a shaman in an operation theatre. We were indulging in some old ritual, some practice devised more for us than for her.

Em made a full recovery. The growth was large but benign and in order to prevent any recurrence, they took out her ovaries as well.

'Just call me the Female Eunuch,' she laughed, as she pulled on her first beedi in three weeks.

'Do you really mind?' Sue asked.

'I don't know. I'll let you know,' said Em, in a rare moment of uncertainty about her own feelings. 'But right now, they're saying I'm over with menstruation and I can only say, Callooh-Callay! If the hot flushes and emotional instability start, that's another matter. Who wants a hot flush? Who wants emotional instability? It sounds like something from a Mills & Boon, and at the wrong end of my life, too. And now, we can have sex without worrying about the consequences.'

She never alluded to it after that. I remember wondering if she would be calmer now. When I was growing up no one ever talked about PMS or anything like that, so this was not a scientific thing. It was some atavistic throwback to the time when hysteria was believed to be seated in the uterus. And since science will eventually win through, we never did see a change in her cycles after her hysterectomy. She went on being Em. She went on trying to kill herself. So when the old man knocked on the door, one morning in May, we thought the worst.

Susan answered the imperious knocking.

'Your mother,' said the old man.

Susan went from bleary-eyed to alert. She woke me and I woke The Big Hoom and we ran down into the street. Em was lying in the street, a bottle of milk shattered close to her arm, which was awkwardly bent next to her.

'It wasn't me,' she said and smiled before she passed out.

We carried her home, The Big Hoom and I, and then we called Dr Saha.

'Broken,' said Dr Saha, who had learnt that words were not much use when diagnoses were needed.

'Fracture?' The Big Hoom asked.

'Broken,' said Dr Saha again. I had always thought it was the same thing. It wasn't. A broken arm required surgery and a pin to be put in and another scar running down Em's arm.

'He came at me like a bat out of hell,' she said later. 'I always look left, look right, and all that. But then there he was –' She stopped abruptly. 'The milk bottle?'

Milk bottles were precious things back then. You couldn't get milk out of the rationing system if you didn't produce your bottle, nicely washed.

'It's all right,' Susan said.

'Liar,' said Em. 'How could it have survived? I felt it fly out of my hand and then I was out like a light. Anyway, I appreciate the thought.'

We all knew what that meant. She would remember that bottle for years. She would worry about the loss of it when she was depressed and it would translate into a new worry about what we would eat and who would cook it. Her mind was like that: a sponge for troubles. Events turned into omens; carelessly uttered phrases into mantras.

But as she aged, the process of accretion, the rate of accretion slowed down.

'It's age,' Dr Michael said. 'The highs will get lower; the lows won't be that bad.'

We couldn't see it but we clung to this hope; that things were getting better. And maybe they were, for three full years passed without her trying to kill herself. Then, suddenly, death turned around and claimed her.

13.

'The last great mystery'

I was spending the night at a friend's home when he called. We had gone to watch a film, we had had a nice meal. Em was going through a manic phase but with both Susan and The Big Hoom in attendance, I was allowed out of the house. I did not sleep that night; I never did in anyone else's home. It was too much of a novelty and I wanted to savour every moment of it. I told this to Susan once and she said, 'I go to sleep almost immediately at sleepovers. It's so nice not to worry.'

When the phone rang in another home, for some reason, I knew it was for me.

'She's gone,' he said and his voice seemed to have no emotion in it, a dry shell where once a rich and milky grain had been.

'Did she . . . ?'

But I found I could not ask whether she had killed herself.

'No,' he said.

It was too early to disturb my hosts. I left quietly, and when I stepped out of the building there was even a part of me that enjoyed the cool breath of the half-night upon my face. The taxi home sliced through the suburbs, over roads free of traffic. Here and there, the bodies of other Mumbaikars lay, in what looked like positions of death. And then I was in Mahim, so quickly, I hadn't even thought about this. What did it mean? Em not around?

'The last great mystery,' she had called it, often.

'If anyone should have some clues, it should be you,' I had said, once.

She had chuckled.

'If only that were so. But at least it holds no fears for me. Bring it on, I say.'

Here, then, it was.

The door was wide open when I got into the flat, light pouring out, the universal sign of death. Inside, all was noise and commotion. I ducked into the bedroom where Em lay on the bed with Susan sitting by her side. Silent, unmoving, there was something very wrong about her. Very wrong. I still don't know how else to describe it. From my reading of crime novels, I knew all about the changes in the body after death, how the muscles let go, how the tension goes out of the body, the pooling of body fluids, the tiny explosions within each cell.

The Big Hoom came out and hugged me briefly. I could not remember this happening often. But she did not die often and things did not fall apart often. The centre did not stop holding often. Did it take death?

'What happened?'

'It was a heart attack,' he said. I almost smiled. A heart attack? Those happened to other people. My mother could not have died of a heart attack.

Susan seemed to read my thoughts.

'It's true. He woke up and found her curled up beside him.'

I sat down beside her. I wanted to hug her but I couldn't. We didn't hug. Em did the hugging. She ambushed people with hugs and kisses. Potchie kisses she called them when she left a bit of saliva behind.

'Odd,' I said.

'Not with a bang but not even a whimper.'

There had been both, bangs and whimpers. But she had left in silence, in sleep.

The world came back in. Other people, their voices, their curious faces, their odd movements. We were not used to other people. We went to see them; they did not come to see us. They did not want to see her and she was uneasy with them until she was comfortable. A stray comment could bring with it repercussions that could last for days. Where the visitor sat and what he said and what he did provided rich mulch in which strange fantasies, ribaldries, fears and scenarios could grow. Visitors were not encouraged. No, we didn't have visitors. Now we could. Did we want them? Did we know what to do with them?

I could not believe that I was already . . .

'Have you bathed?' Susan asked.

I had not.

'You should bathe,' Susan said, a trace of elder-sister irritation showing at the edges of her concern. Was I concerned about her? I couldn't tell. I didn't seem to be feeling anything.

I went to shower. The water triggered tears and I wept. When I assumed I had finished, I washed my face again and waited. From time to time, I was startled by a sob rising in me. These did not seem to be linked to the pain I was feeling. They seemed organic, like marsh gas, like breathing.

What was this to be like? How were we to be? There were all kinds of questions to be dealt with and a host of people to deal with them. Did we have a nice dress? (Susan was choosing one.) Would I call the parish priest? (This had already been done.) Who had signed the death certificate? (Dr Saha had asked for someone to come to his house by nine o'clock.) And what kind of coffin would we like? (Like?)

There seemed to be many young men in the room. One of them returned with ice, a huge block of it.

'Where shall I put this?' he asked me, a hunter-gatherer triumphant at having returned with his kill.

'He's the son,' hissed another young man. I did not recognize either one but they both seemed to feel they had the right to be there and to be helpful. It was the badge of their tribe.

'Sorry, aahn?' he said. Obviously the son of the deceased was not expected to be able to answer questions. He took the ice into the kitchen and began to divide it up into blocks.

A series of women came by and kissed me. Granny surfaced suddenly among them, her face tear-streaked and the women changed direction and began to kiss her.

'Rose dress,' said Granny. 'Her rose dress. She thissing.'

Susan got up to find the dress in which Em had said she wanted to be buried. I sat down next to The Big Hoom.

'I thought it would be me,' he said. 'I thought I would go first.'

'I thought so too,' I said. It seemed thoughtless but he didn't seem hurt. I didn't know why I had said such a thing. Perhaps it was only because men die first in Goan Roman Catholic families and their women don black and courage in equal measure and make pickles until their sons become bishops and can give sermons about them. He didn't seem to be paying attention. The air was filling with the smell of lilies as wreaths began to come in. Who was sending these flowers? I couldn't stand the smell of lilies.

'I'm going to the undertaker,' I said.

'Only if your mind is quiet,' he said.

My mind wasn't, but I did remember that Em had declared that she would like to be buried as simply as possible. And that she had wanted to be useful. I went back into the house and intercepted Susan.

'She wanted to donate her eyes.'

'They came and went,' she said.

They took her eyes? Yes, sure, that was what she wanted. I suddenly wanted to see her eyes but I knew that would no longer be possible. It would have to be memory now.

You have your mother's eyes, I had been told often.

I began to cry again but I managed not to sob. You can cry in public as long as you do not sob. Tears are transparent. If you're walking fast, if the sun's too strong, no one notices. Sobs intrude. They push their way into people's consciousness. They feel duty-bound to ask what has happened. I cried silently all the way to the undertaker.

Outside his storefront, the undertaker had a sign: 'We can take your dead body, anywhere, anytime, anyplace.' Visually, this was represented by an aeroplane with a coffin dangling from it. Later, the undertaker would become something of a minor celebrity for his signboards. 'When you drop dead, drop in,' one would say. The next one said, 'Mr Smoker, you're the next one to come coffin in.' This was followed by 'We're the last to let you down.' And then would come the strange 'Grave problems resurrected here.'

But at the time, there was only a coffin dangling from a plane and three albums full of images of coffins. Some were white ('For nuns, priests, and unmarried people,' said the attendant), but most were wood-brown or purple. There was a bewildering variety of images, and a range of designs. The man kept up a steady litany, '. . . lace pillow with real silk, or you can have satin pillow, handmade fittings on the side, brass or you can go for this one which has silver, but first you want to decide what you want, teak or plain. But do you have a permanent grave?'

I had no idea but I was guessing we didn't.

'No good. Got to know.'

I called home. We didn't.

'Ah good. Sometimes problem like that comes. You done the booking?'

I had no idea what we were supposed to book.

'You go tell the faaders. Or we can tell. But you made up your mind?'

When it became apparent that I did not want a slow-moving hearse or a teak coffin lined with real silk, the undertaker lost interest in the proceedings. He told me what I had to do and left me to do it.

At home, the women of the family had finished washing the body. They had dressed her up and put cheerful pink shoes on her feet.

A priest arrived, looking a bit bedraggled. He was served tea and began a rosary. Afterwards, he blessed the body and came and asked me if I wanted to speak. I had no idea what to say. I could have put the words together but then I had no idea whether I would be able to get through them. And I knew that if they were glib and born out of a need to impress, they would come back to haunt me. So we opted for a service that would in no way suggest how unique Em had been or how powerful a force she had been in our lives. The ordinary words would cloak her remains in the normal. There would be no reminders of who she was and how different her life had been or how strange our grief was.

After the funeral, we went home.

Susan went off to take a nap. The Big Hoom continued to behave as he had all day, as if a large part of his personality was dissolving and he was unable to stop it. The wake was an ordinary one. After the initial moments of silence and unease, a ten-minute grace period during which the quietness admitted the presence of death, human nature reasserted itself: conversations began, jokes were exchanged, food was eaten and commented upon, generally unfavourably. The Big Hoom rose, somewhere around an hour into the proceedings, and went into the bedroom. I followed him in. He sat down on the edge of the bed. I helped him off with his coat. He smiled briefly and then lay down.

'I'm all right,' he said. 'Go.'

His voice sounded odd, as if it were coming through something thick and viscous. I left him alone to grieve. Susan moved through people with an assurance that seemed new and somewhat overweening, as if she were preparing for the role of family matriarch already. In her hands, and it seemed as if she had an unending supply of them, trays of sandwiches appeared, and individual cups of tea – no sugar, touch of milk; two sugars and generous milk – found their way to the small islands of teetotallers among the bibulous crowd. Granny was surrounded by dowagers, all of whom looked mildly envious of her state. They didn't seem to be saying much, just sighing at each other and letting clichés drop into the silence.

'She's at peace now, poor dear.'

'Who can understand God's will?'

'Whatever it is, she had a heart of gold.'

Cigarette smoke began to cloud the room. And slowly death, the notion of death, departed. The sounds began to take the shape of a party.

For a moment, I felt a huge panic, a suffocating hatred for my own kind, a need to remind all those present that they too would die. In other words, I felt like making a scene or running away or both. Of course, I stayed on and said nothing. I dipped my head and let various women leave traces of talcum powder, liquid foundation and lipstick on my cheek. I shook hands and hugged a series of men, each leaving behind a signature odour. When it became clear that the last of the whiskey had been served and no more was forthcoming, the wake began to fall asleep.

Then the last straggler departed and we were alone. Home was already a thinner, lighter space. There had been days when I had felt suffocated by the life we lived in that flat. I had imagined then that the time would come when I would be the sole owner of these four hundred and twenty square feet of real estate. I remember planning how it would happen. First Susan would get married. Then The Big Hoom would die. And an ugly thrill would run through me at the thought. It was composed of real fear at the thought of his death, of horror at myself at imagining such things, of amazement at the sheer perversity of realizing that this was the only way I would get what I wanted. Then it would be down to me and Em. She would be a problem, but I would manage it so well that everyone – a mythic multi-tongued million-eyed all-knowing Everyone – would praise my handling of my responsibilities while tut-tutting at my reputation as a ladies' man but admitting tight-lipped that I was a genius at my profession, whatever that should be.

And then Em too would die and I would be alone and the whole world would be different. I had no idea how, but it would be, because I would finally have space to myself and then I could exercise the choice to do as I pleased and when I pleased instead of waiting for a stolen moment in the busy life of this 1BHK.

And now the world expanded as people left the flat. As we opened the door together, I discovered that departures make the world smaller, slighter, less significant. For a moment, my father and I and Susan looked at each other.

Survivors, I thought. Shipwreck survivors.

'Tea?' I asked.

He nodded wordlessly and I followed Susan into the kitchen. She set out four cups. I put one away. She began to weep silently. She had always wept silently. And she had always wanted to be alone to weep, so I left the kitchen.

When I returned to the hall, The Big Hoom was sitting in the single armchair and crying too.

My first thought was, 'Oh God.' My second thought was, 'Susan should deal with this.' But neither God nor Susan would. I was on the spot and it was my call. So I knelt by his side and tried awkwardly to hug him. He tried to stop crying and failed. We stayed like that, with odd thoughts running through my head. 'She was my mother too, damn it' and 'This would be easier on a sofa' and 'Where is that tea?'.

Finally, the tea was ready and it lay there in front of us. I tried to remember if I liked tea or not. I just drank it. It was something we did. It was something Em did.

The Big Hoom looked at his cup and said, 'I think we need something stronger.'

I was not trying to be funny but since we had never kept alcohol in the house, I asked, 'Coffee?'

'No,' he said. 'I want a drink. Go and get us a bottle of Old Monk.'

He began to dig in his pockets for money as if he had forgotten I was now earning money of my own and could buy us a bottle. But something told me to wait and finally he found the small, neat wad of notes and papers secured by a rubber band that served as his wallet. From it, he drew out a couple of notes. He looked at them slightly puzzled. 'Will this be enough, do you think?' he asked.

I grinned at him.

'I think,' I said.

The city continued on its way. Boys tried to sell me drumsticks, girls played hopscotch, the Bihari badli worker carried his gathri of ironed clothes to the homes from which they had come, and the buses honked at suicidal cyclists. At one level this was vaguely confusing. Surely, something should acknowledge how much things had changed? At another level, it was oddly comforting.

When I got back, The Big Hoom was boiling peanuts in brine.

'To go with the rum,' he said. Susan was looking slightly suspicious.

I ordered a garlic chicken dry from the Chinese thela

down the road and found it had gone all swanky. The dish came wrapped in foil instead of the usual thin plastic packet. When I held out the money, the boy looked abashed.

'Uncle ko bolo, free.'

Then he dashed off. This was The City, India's biggest, a huge city, but people heard and responded to what was happening in your life. Sometimes, this much was enough.

Susan was annoyed when I dumped the parcel on the counter.

'There's loads of food already.'

That was when I noticed how much food there was: casseroles and covered dishes and hotpots of it. The Big Hoom looked at it too. Then he went and dug out all the white plastic containers that restaurants use for takeaways.

'What are you doing?' Susan asked. She liked her white plastic containers.

The Big Hoom said quietly, 'This is too much food. I'm giving it away.'

And so all three of us settled down to dividing up the spoils: some carbohydrates, some meat, some vegetables into each one. It gave us something to do. Me, carbs. Susan, meat. The Big Hoom, veg. When we were finished, there were about twenty mini-meals packed and ready.

'I'm going to clean up,' said Susan. 'You two go.'

By acting cautiously, we managed to prevent any food scuffles, though there was one moment of Bombay bizarreness when an old woman asked if we had a vegetarian option. The Big Hoom was polite; I was not.

'Beggars can't be choosers,' I said.

'Did a beggar coin that phrase?' The Big Hoom asked.

'Probably not.'

'Then let's assume that some choices are left, even to beggars.'

'It just sounds so bizarre. I haven't eaten for three days. I'm so hungry. But I won't eat your dirty non-veg food.'

'Suppose she had an allergy? What if it had been an allergy to meat? Would that make it better?'

'Do the poor have allergies?'

We got home to the peanuts and the rum and the garlic chicken dry, none of which looked particularly appetizing.

'One more beggar run?' I asked

'I wonder if there are any teetotal beggars,' Susan said.

'Let's start with a small one each,' I said and we settled down to eat and drink. Susan filled her glass with cola and spiked it with a homoeopathic quantity of rum. I made The Big Hoom's small but he drank it circumspectly after the first big gulp.

'I seem to have lost my taste for this,' he sighed, looking into his glass.

I went to make us some tea.

PP Ro+ 4/16
GT 10/16
TR MN 4/17